PJ MASKS

PJ MASKS SAVE THE DAYTIME!

Licensed by:

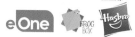

SIMON SPOTLIGHT
An imprint of Simon & Schuster Children's Publishing Division
1230 Avenue of the Americas, New York, New York 10020
This Simon Spotlight edition August 2021
Adapted by Patty Michaels from the series PJ Masks
 For information about special discounts for bulk purchases, please contact Simon & Schuster Special Sales at 1-866-506-1949 or business@simonandschuster.com.
Manufactured in the United States of America 0721 LAK
2 4 6 8 10 9 7 5 3 1
ISBN 978-1-5344-9521-0 (hc)
ISBN 978-1-5344-9520-3 (pbk)
ISBN 978-1-5344-9522-7 (ebook)

PJMASKS

PJ MASKS
SAVE THE DAYTIME!

Written by **PATTY MICHAELS**
Illustrated by **PABLO GALLEGO**

Ready-to-Read *GRAPHICS*

Simon Spotlight
New York   London   Toronto   Sydney   New Delhi

HOW TO READ THIS BOOK

The PJ Masks are here to give you some tips on reading this book.

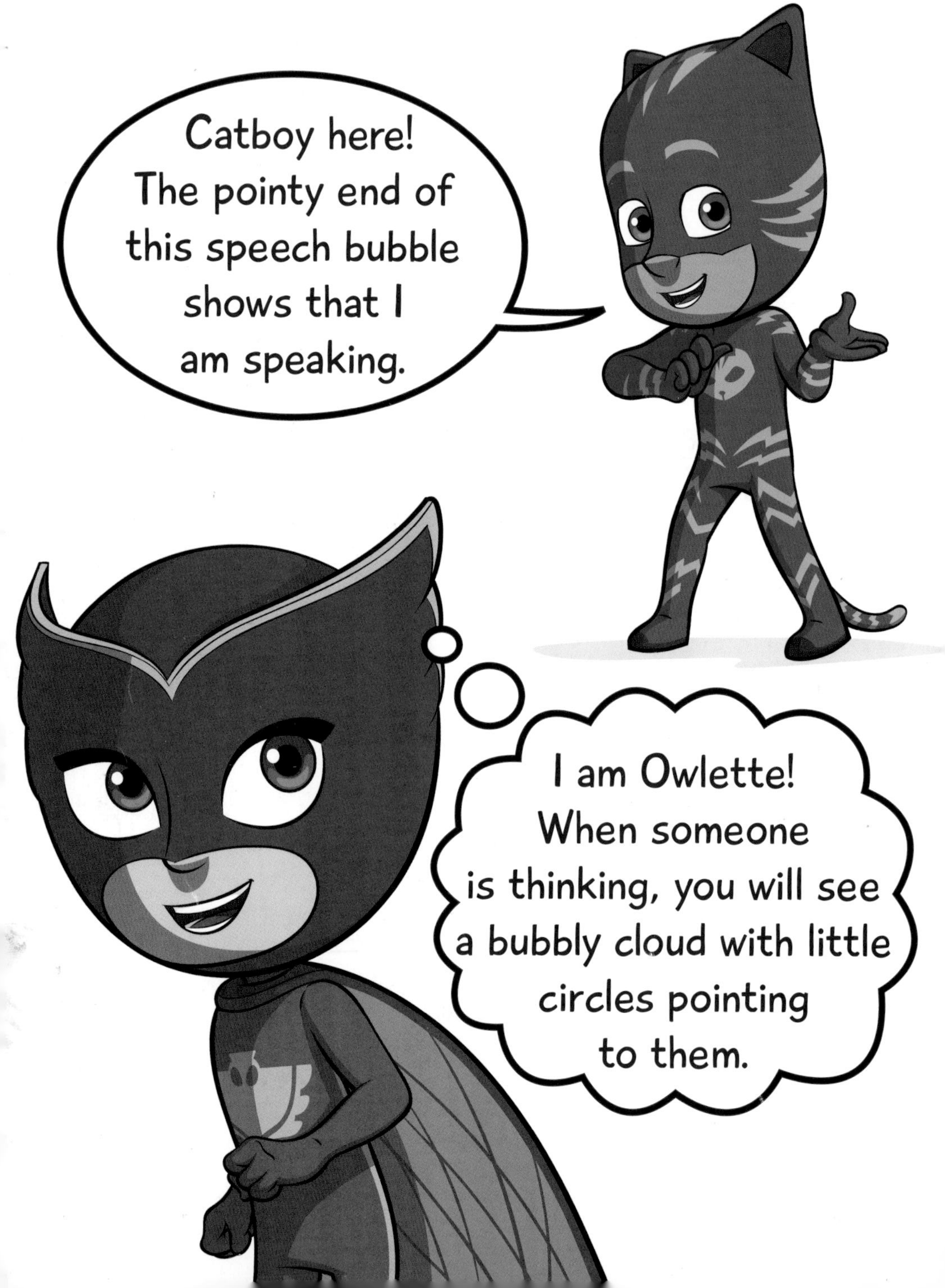
Catboy here! The pointy end of this speech bubble shows that I am speaking.
I am Owlette! When someone is thinking, you will see a bubbly cloud with little circles pointing to them.

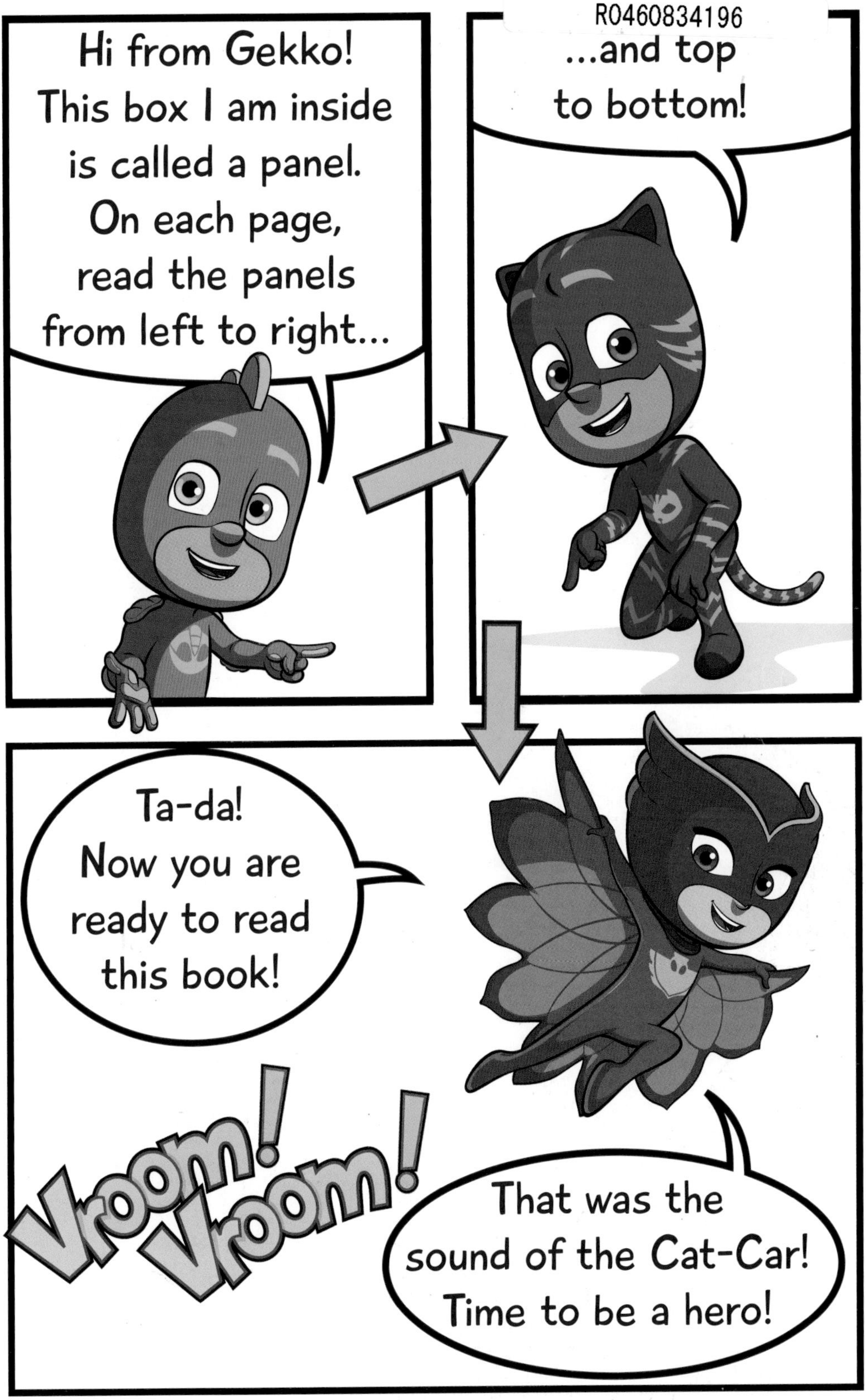
Hi from Gekko! This box I am inside is called a panel. On each page, read the panels from left to right...
...and top to bottom!
Ta-da! Now you are ready to read this book!
Vroom! Vroom!
That was the sound of the Cat-Car! Time to be a hero!

The class is going on a dress-up field trip to the park!

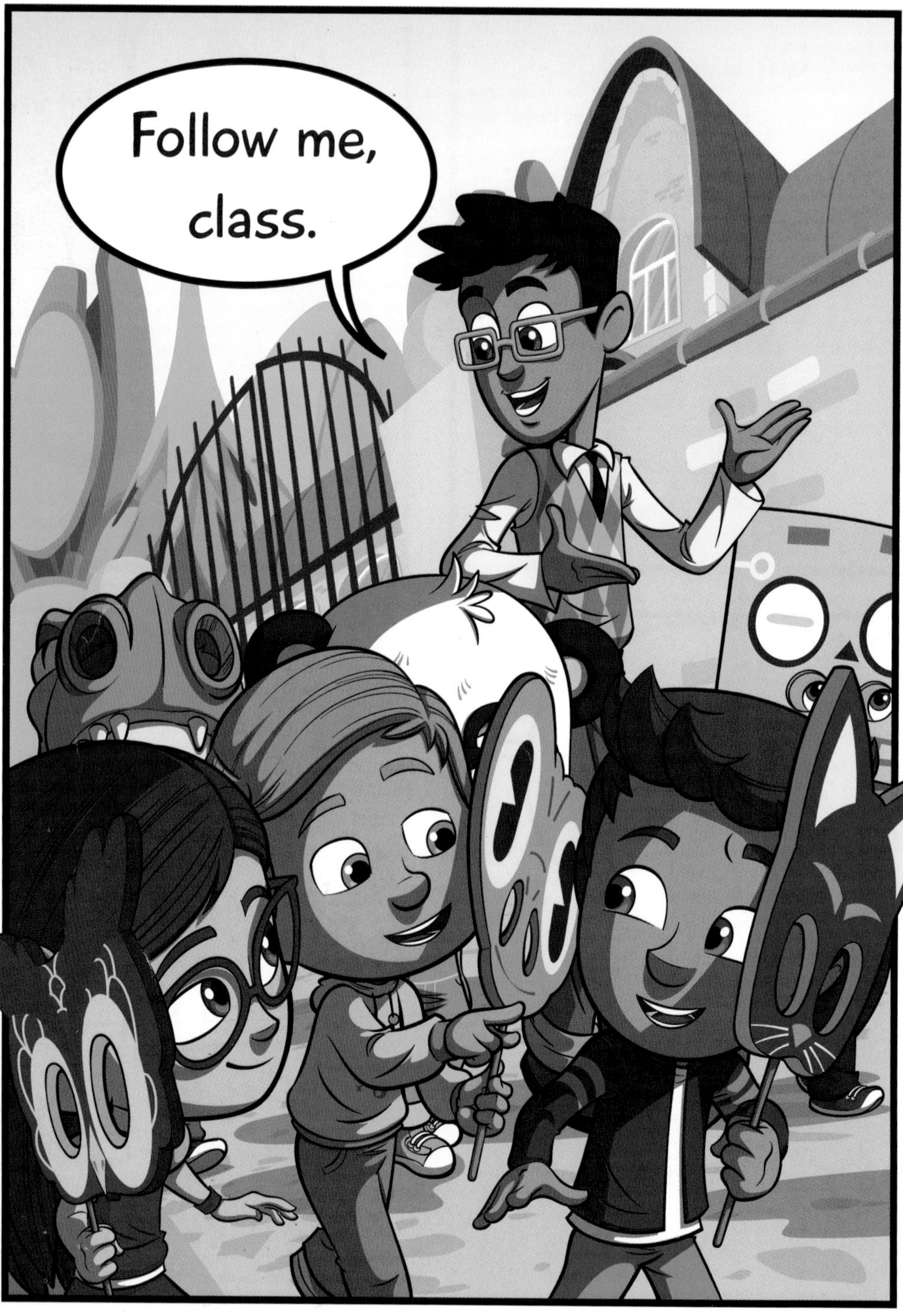
Follow me, class.

In the middle of the day, it becomes...night in the city?

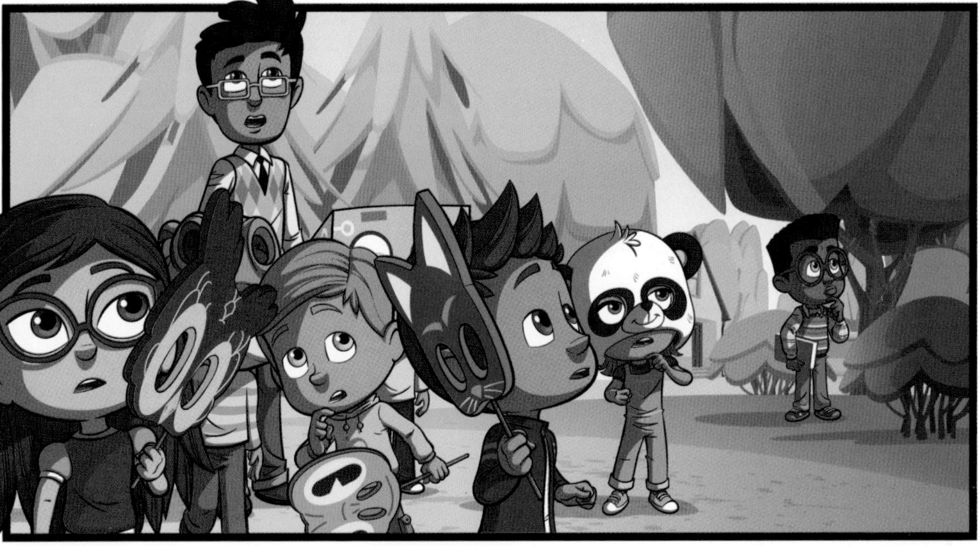

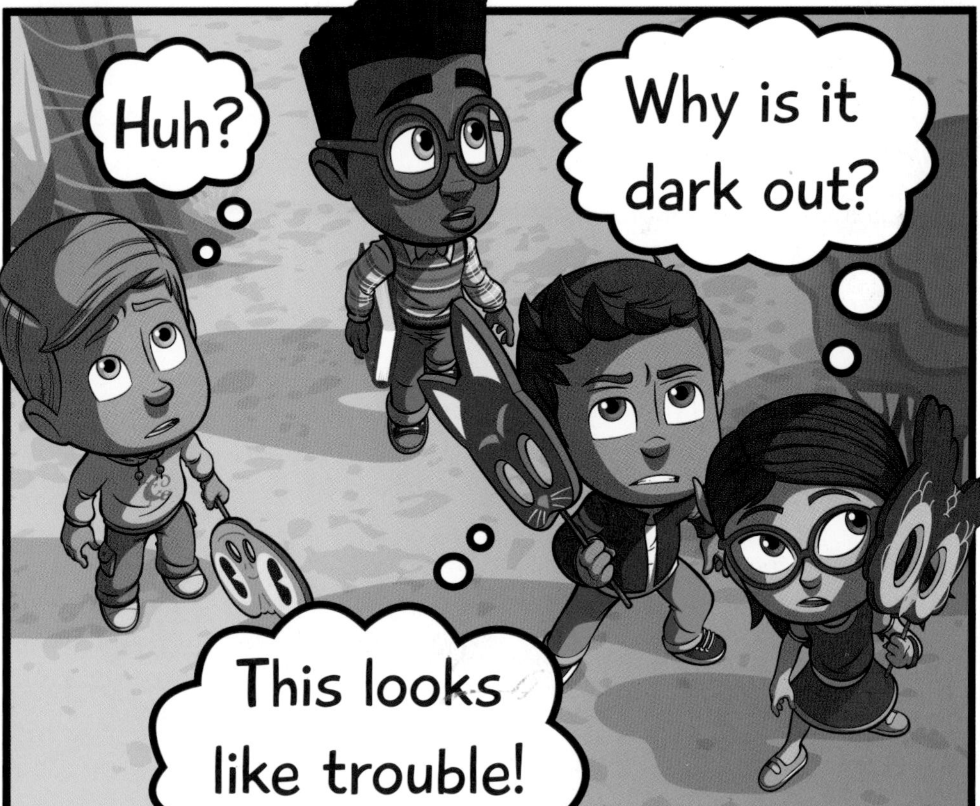
Huh?
Why is it dark out?
This looks like trouble!

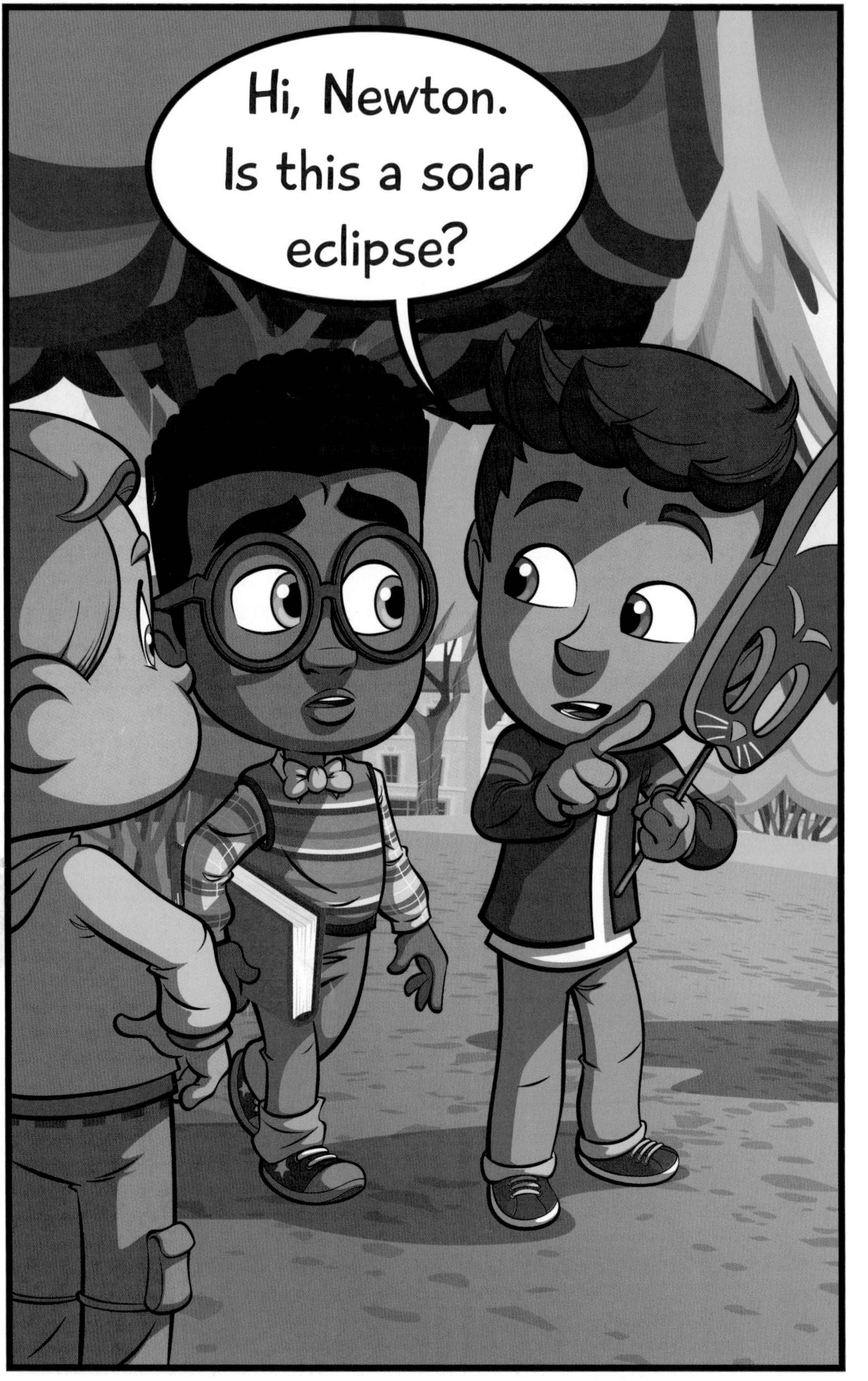
Hi, Newton.
Is this a solar
eclipse?

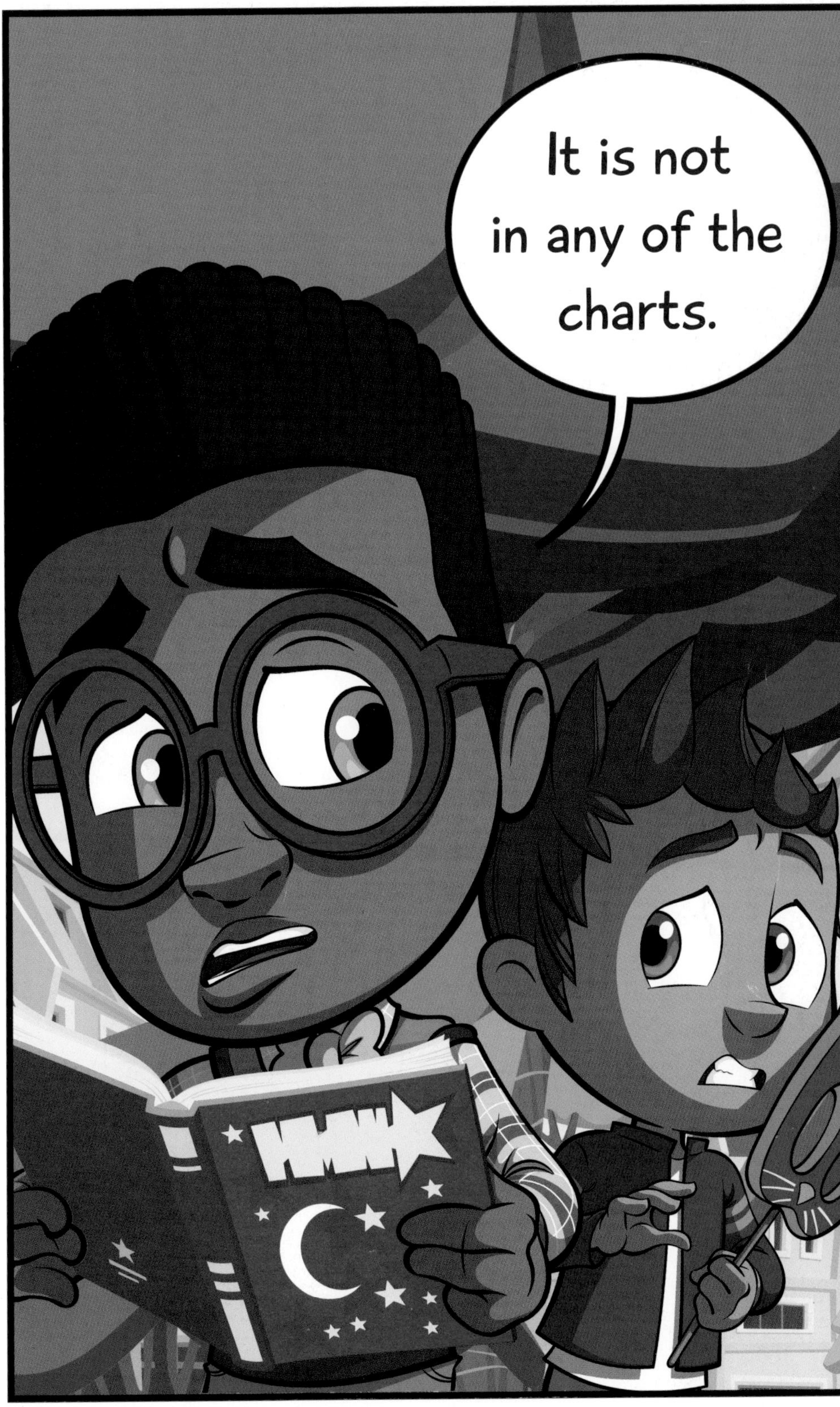
It is not in any of the charts.

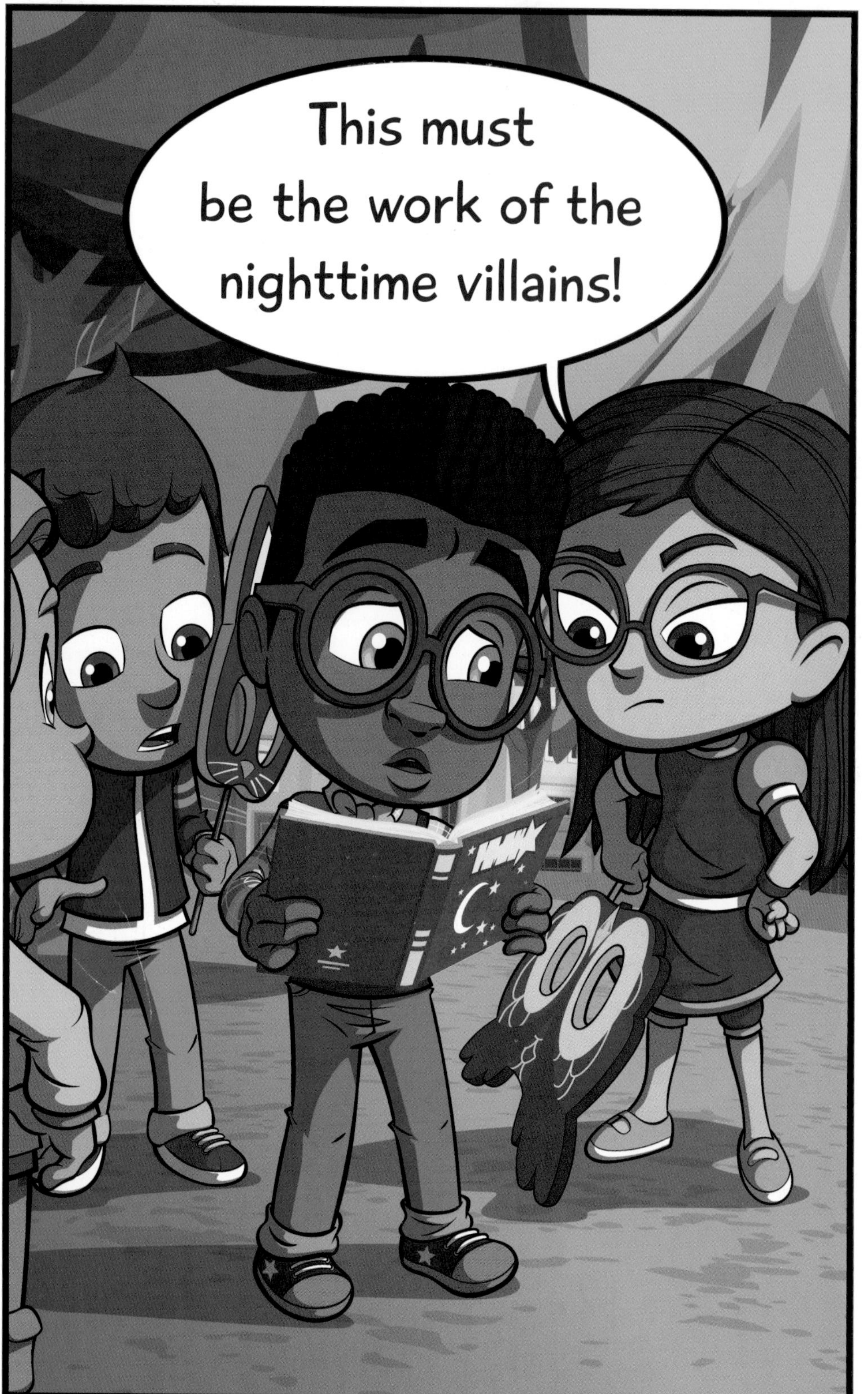
This must be the work of the nighttime villains!

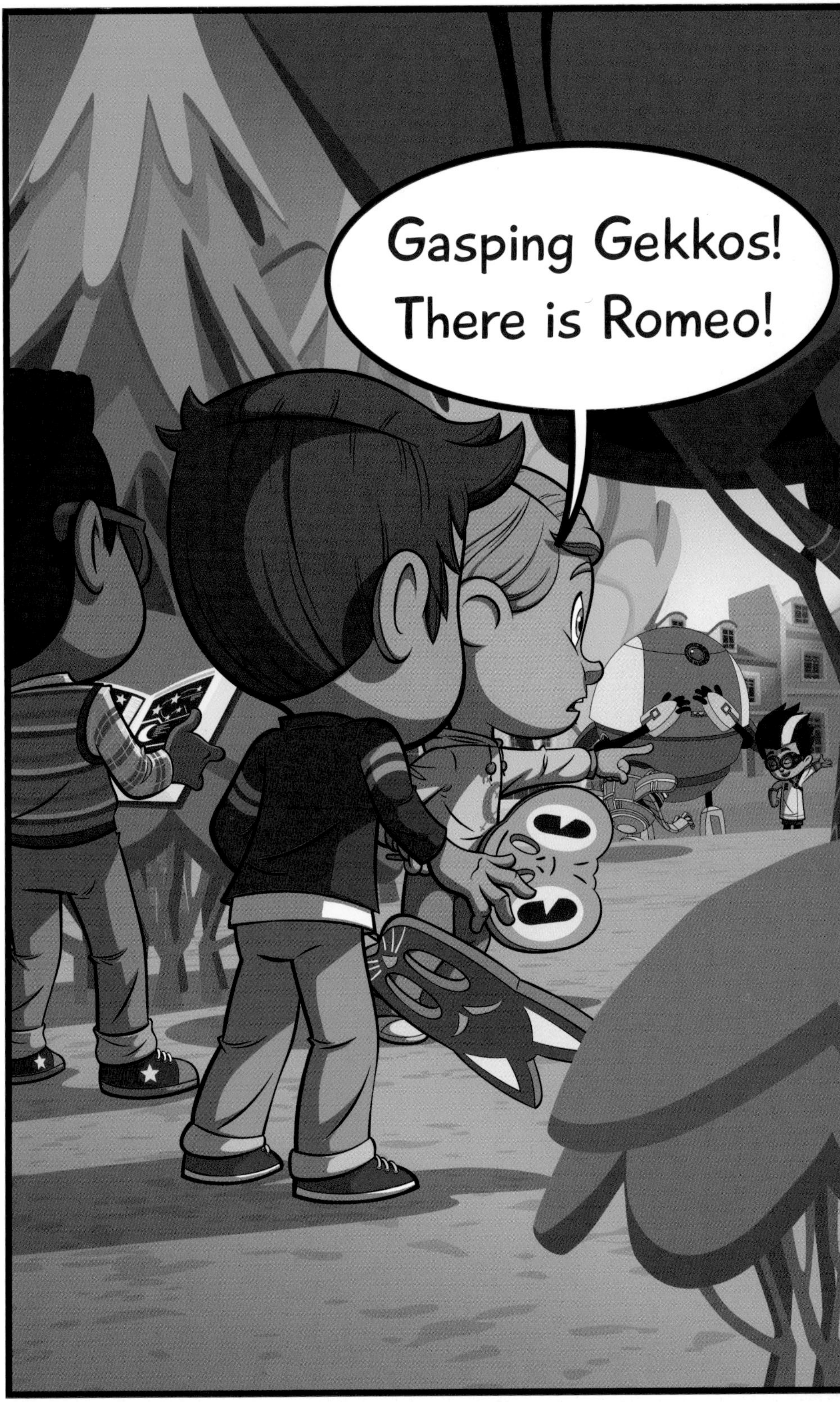
Gasping Gekkos! There is Romeo!

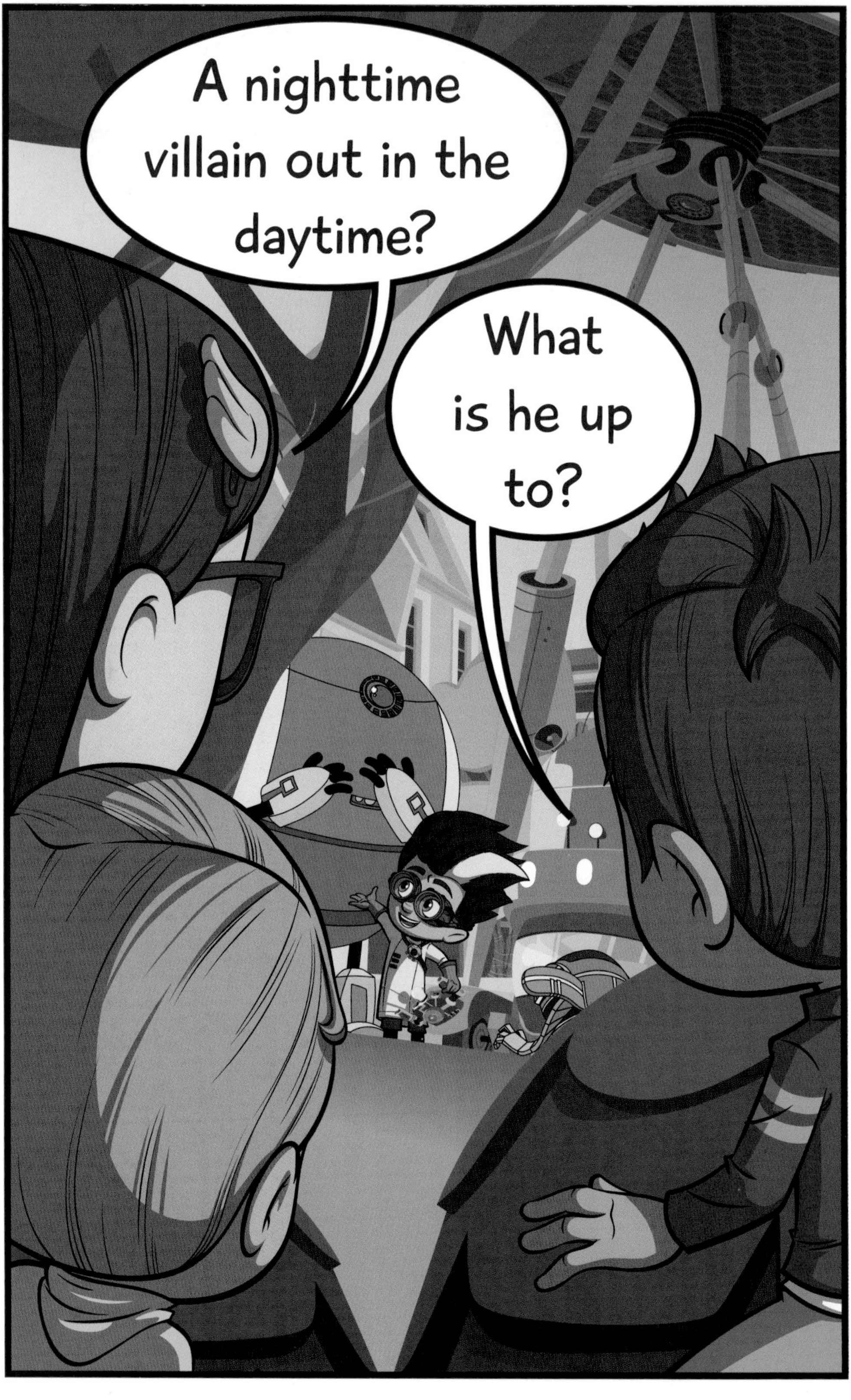
A nighttime villain out in the daytime?
What is he up to?

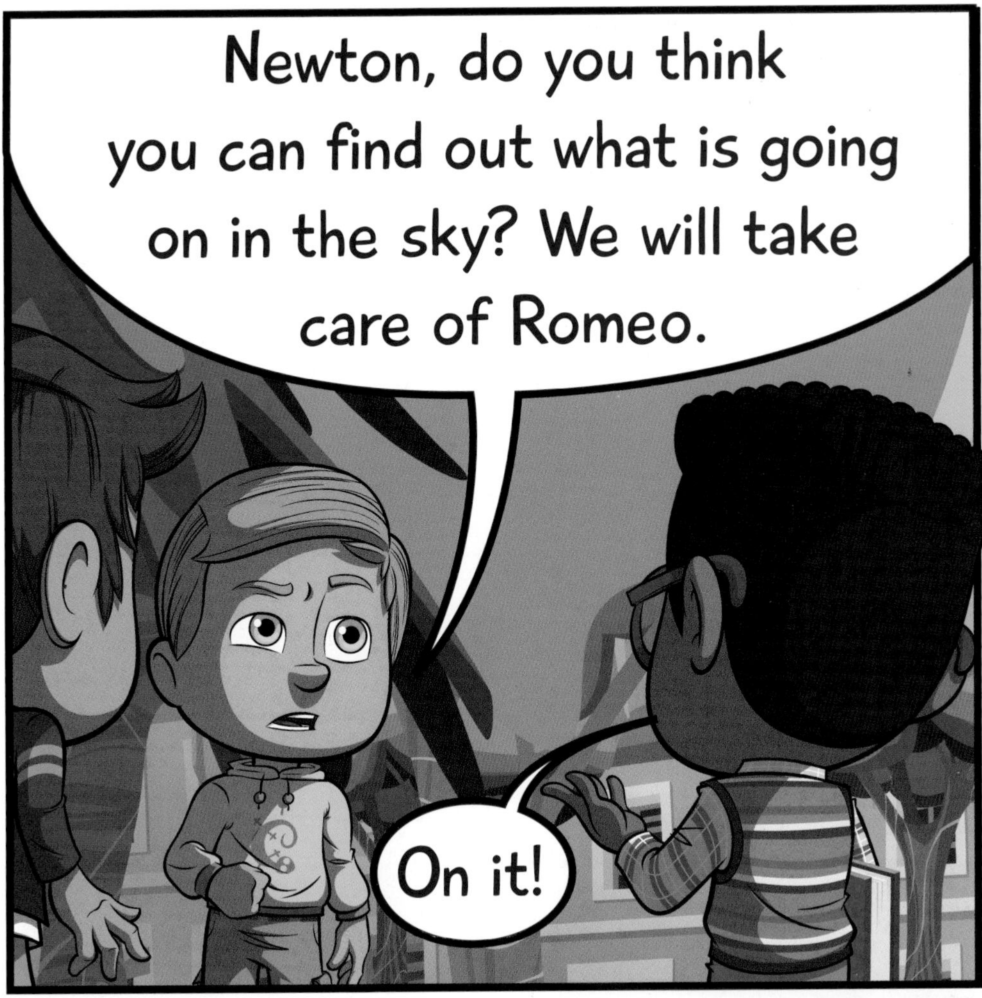
Newton, do you think you can find out what is going on in the sky? We will take care of Romeo.
On it!

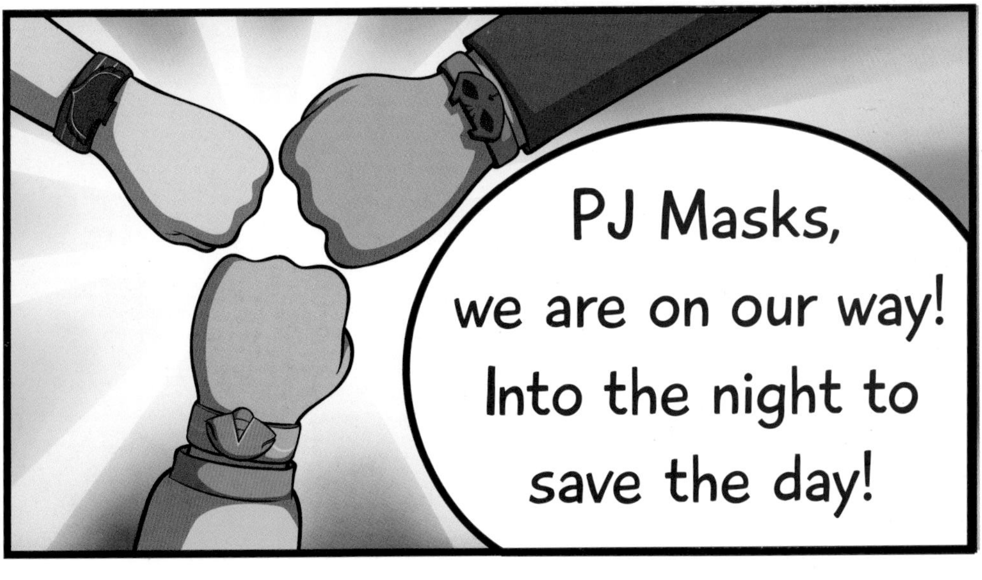
PJ Masks, we are on our way! Into the night to save the day!

Amaya becomes Owlette!

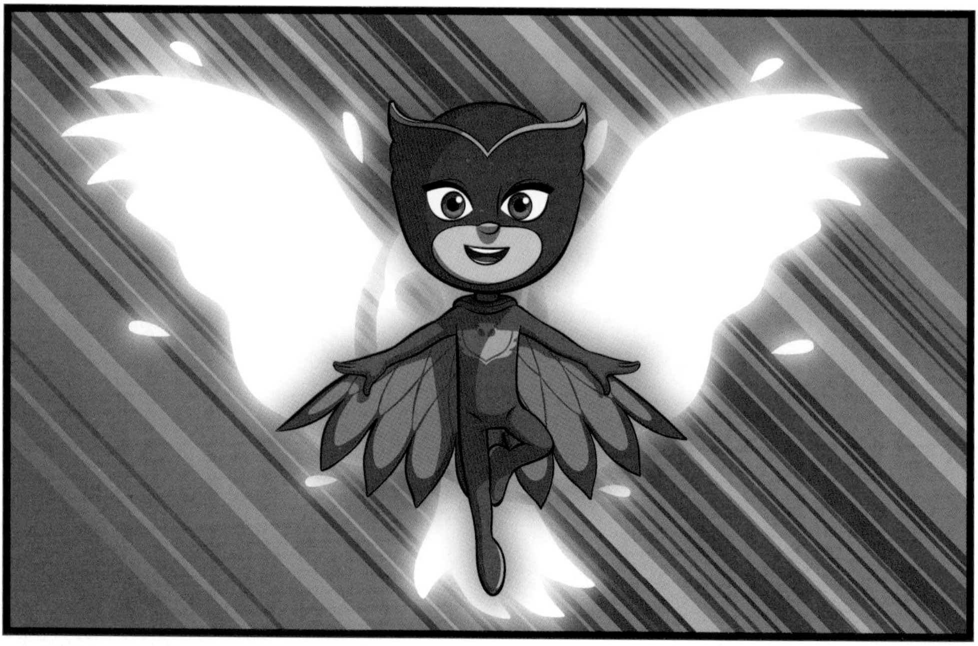

Greg becomes Gekko!

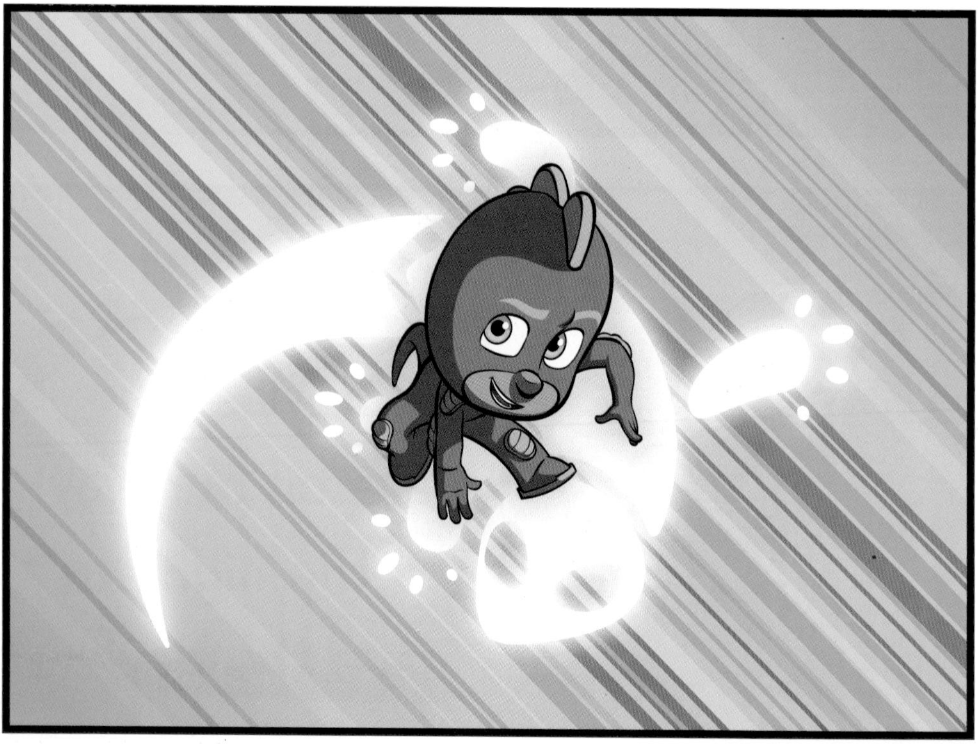

Connor becomes Catboy!

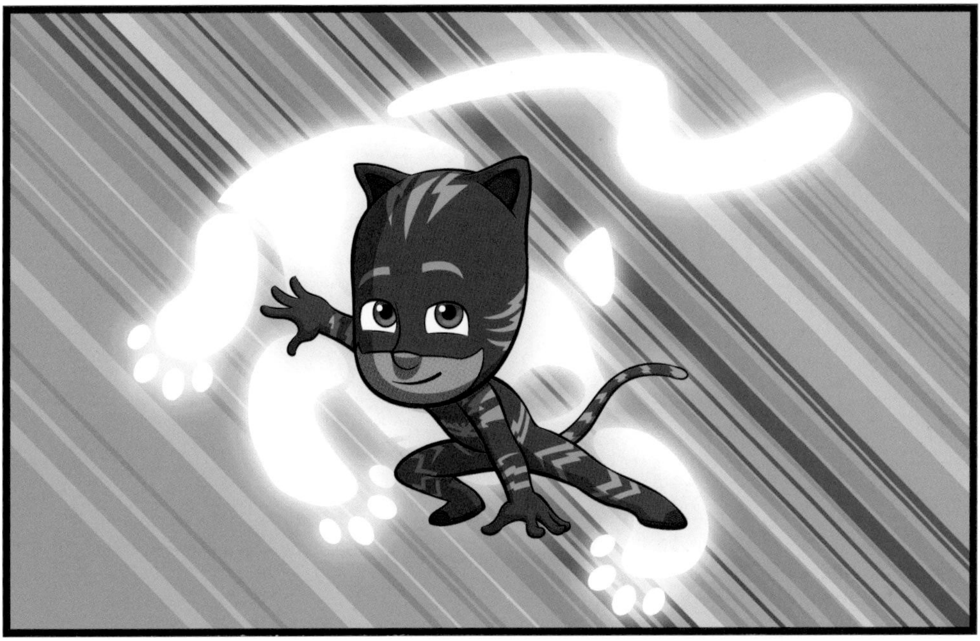

They are the PJ Masks!

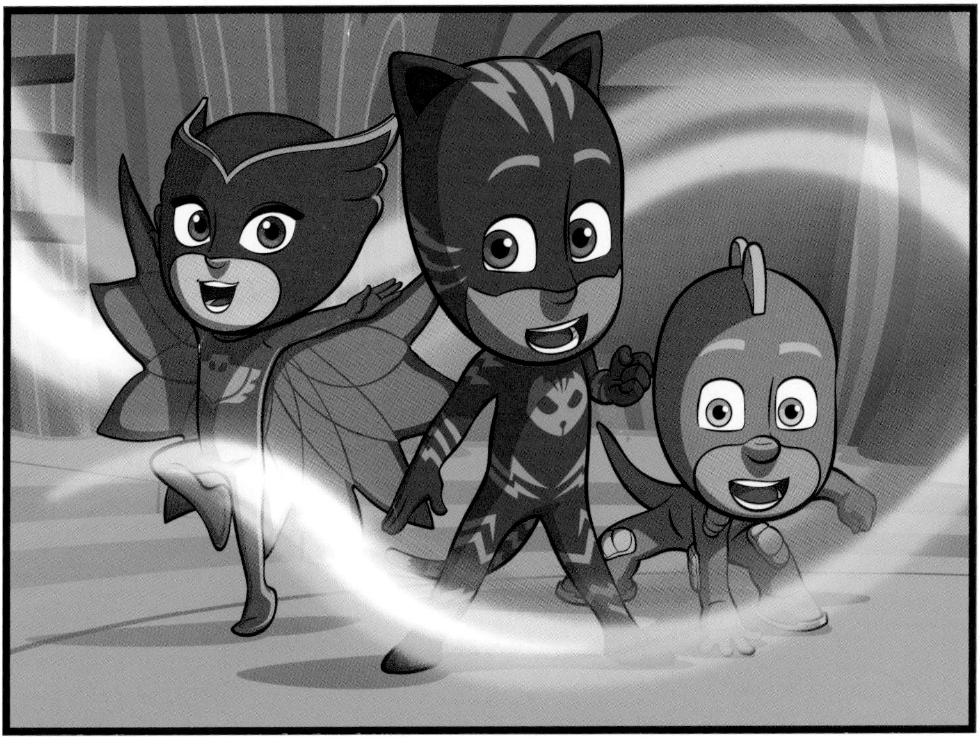

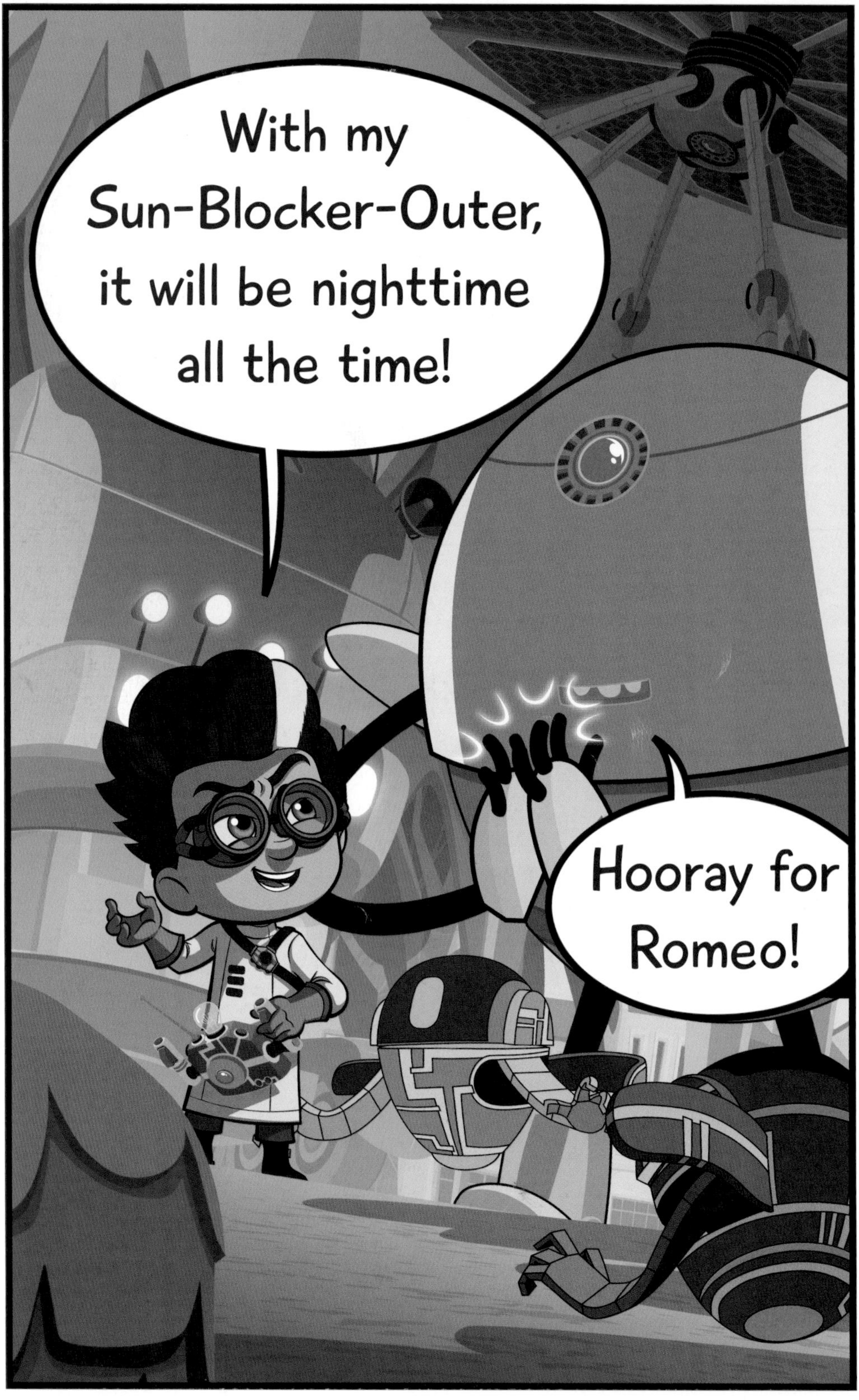
With my Sun-Blocker-Outer, it will be nighttime all the time!
Hooray for Romeo!

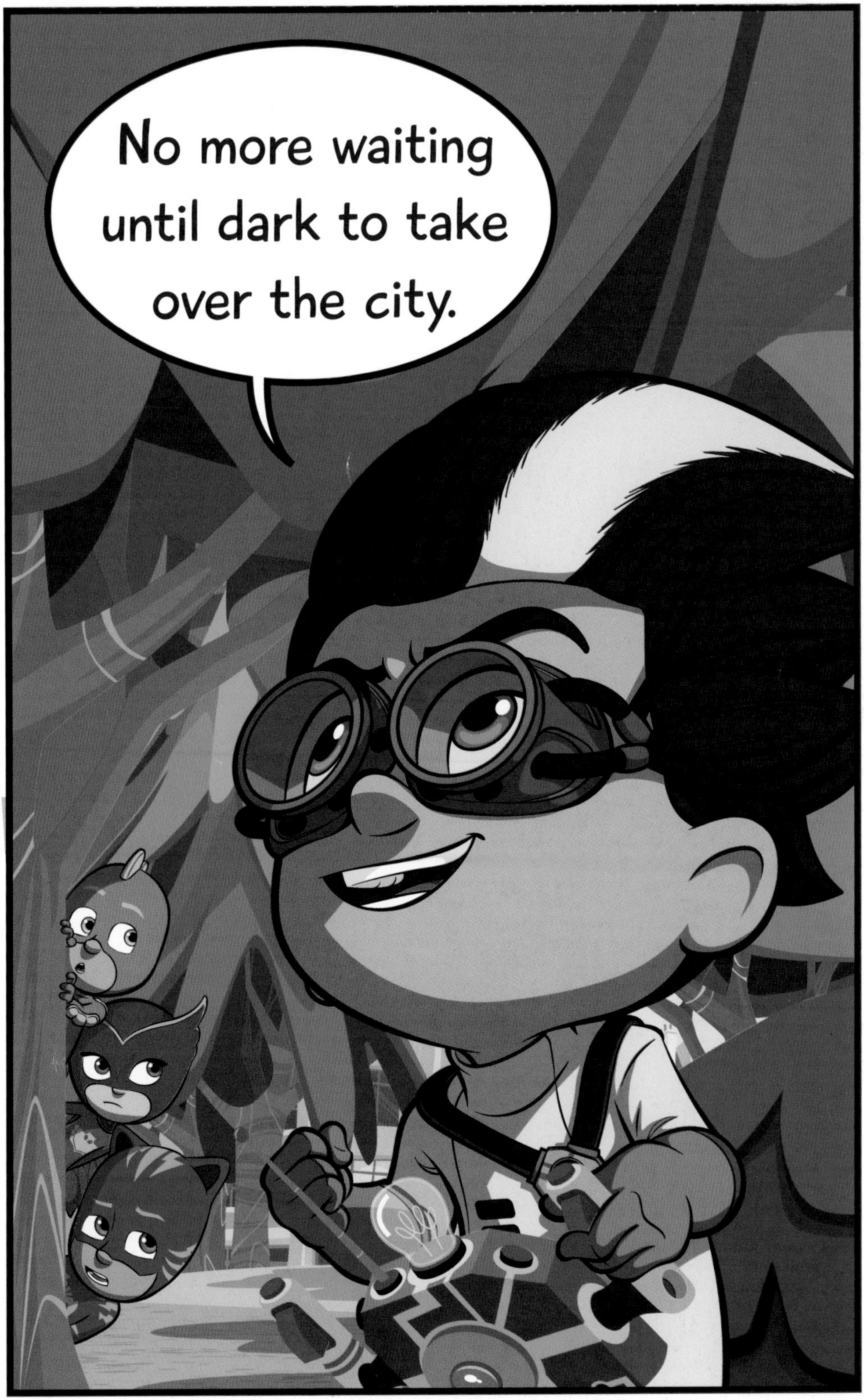
No more waiting until dark to take over the city.

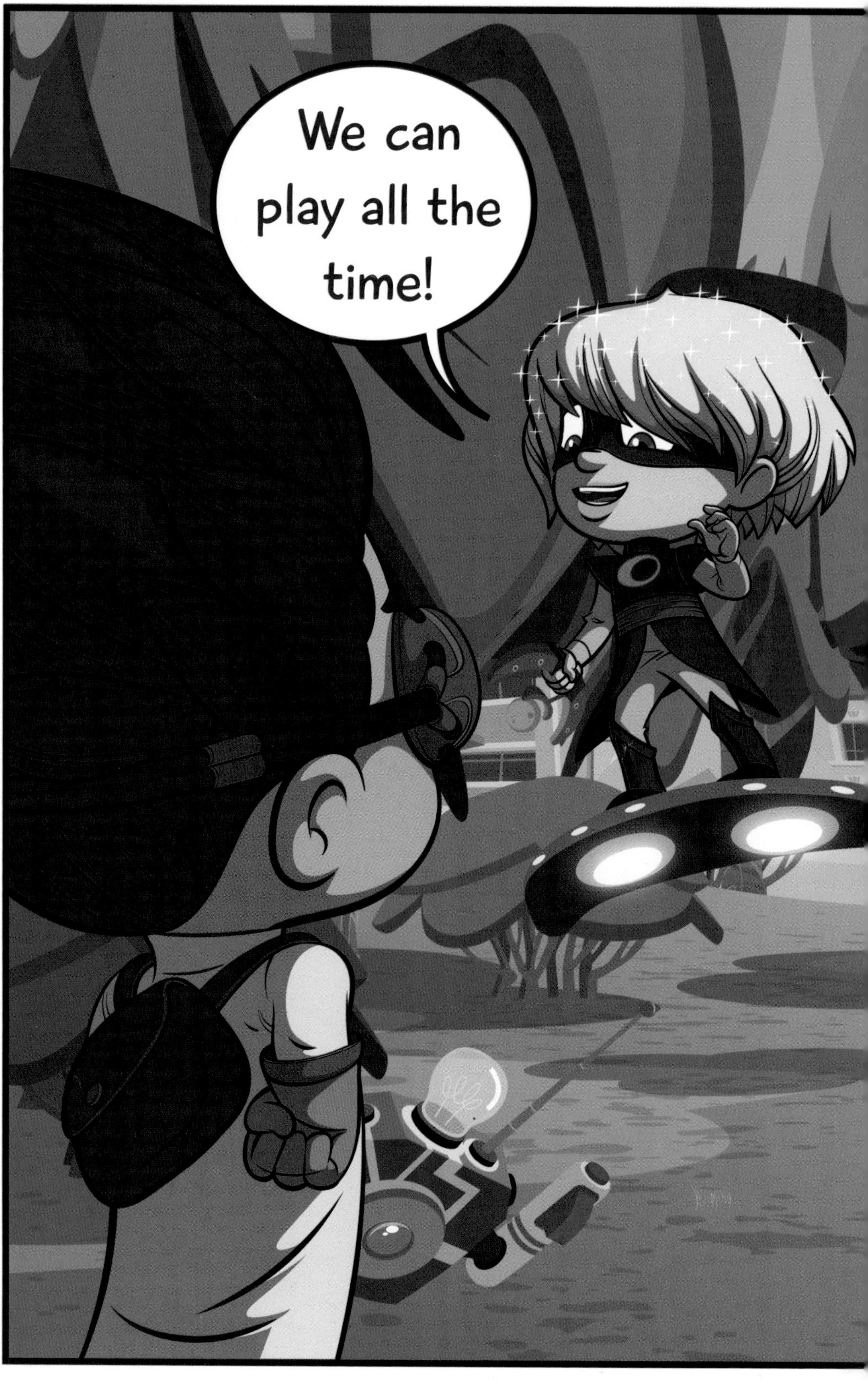
We can play all the time!

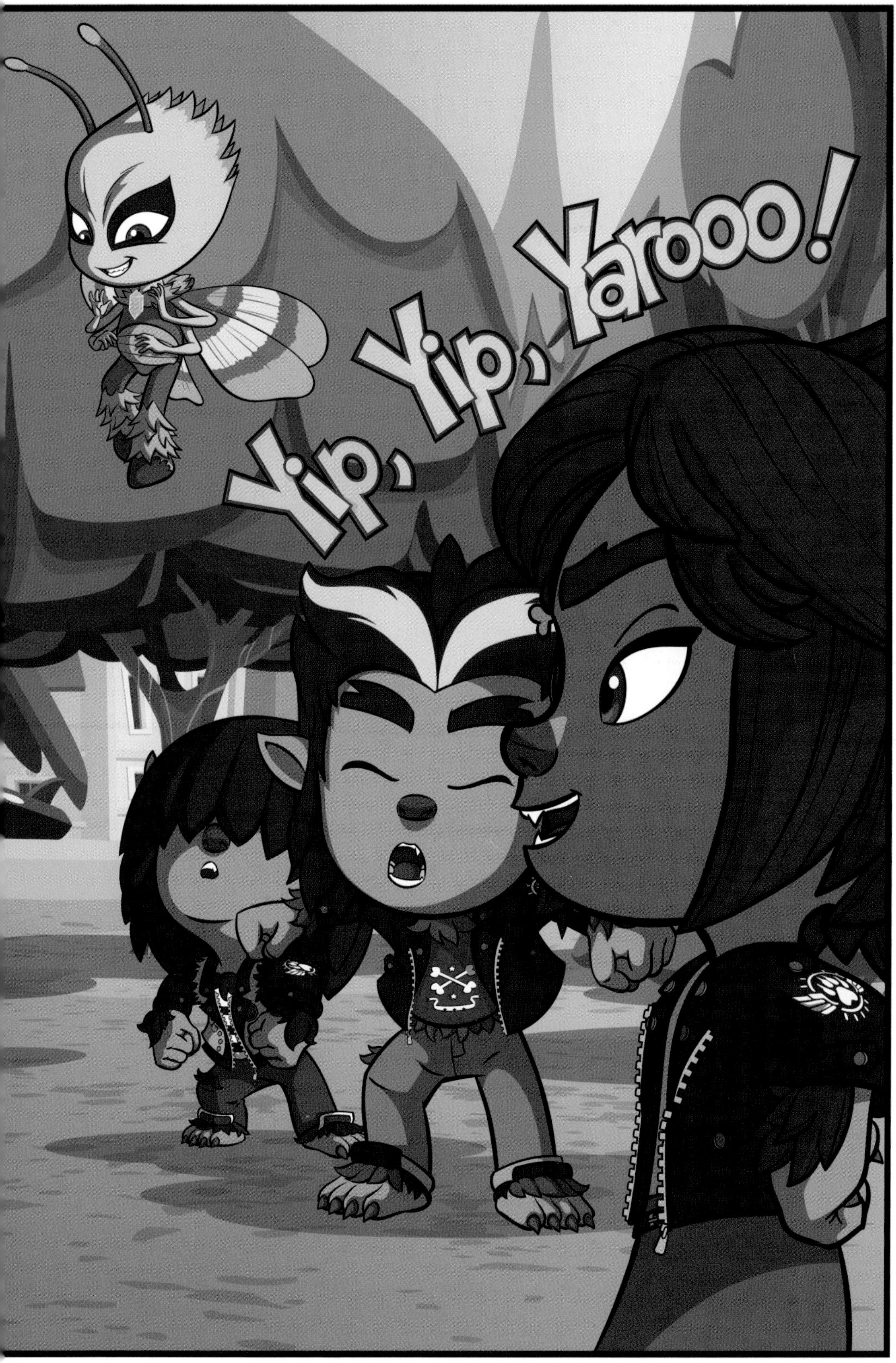
Yip, Yip, Yarooo!

Meanwhile, the school kids were busy playing hide-and-seek.

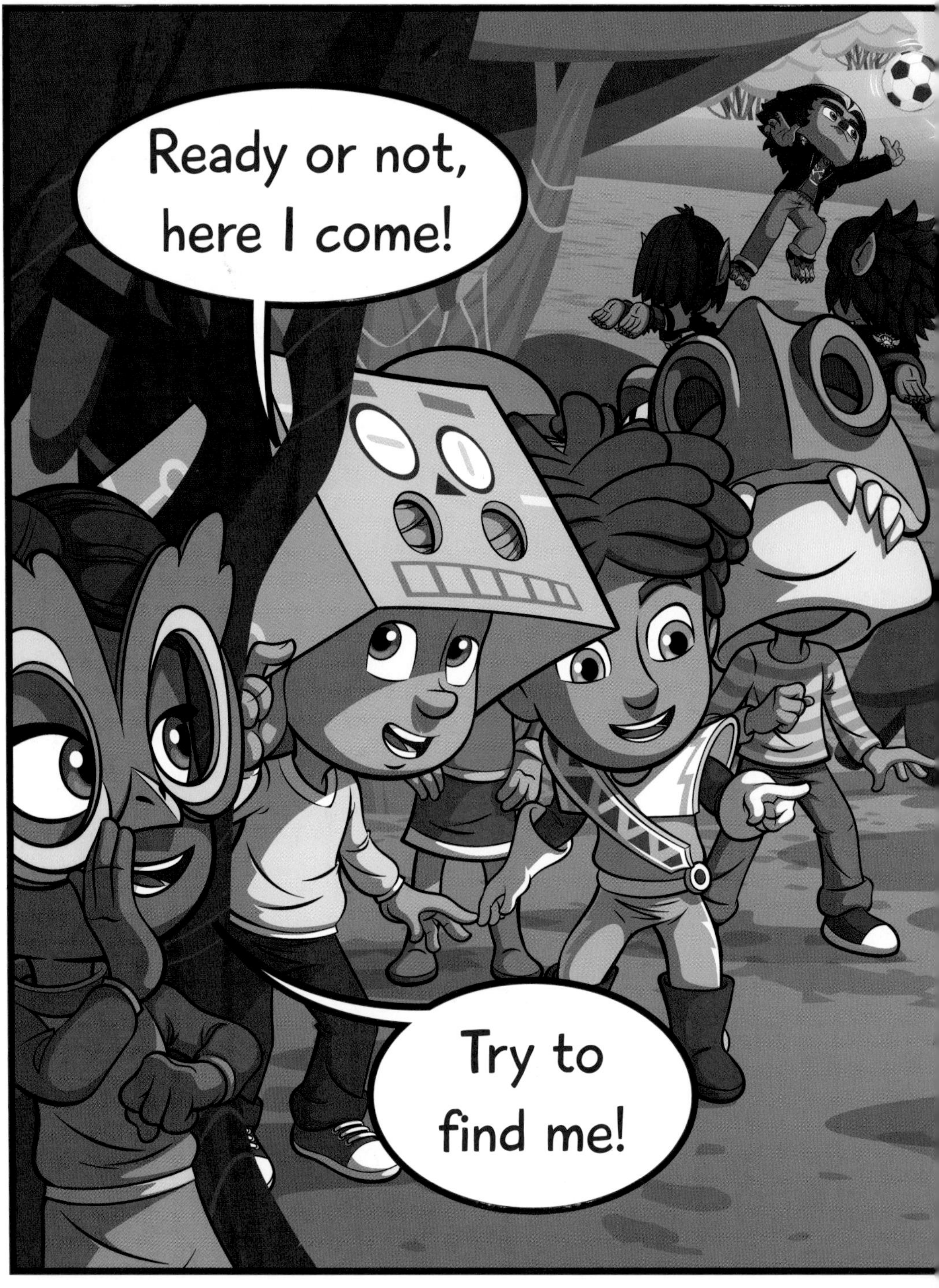
Ready or not, here I come!
Try to find me!

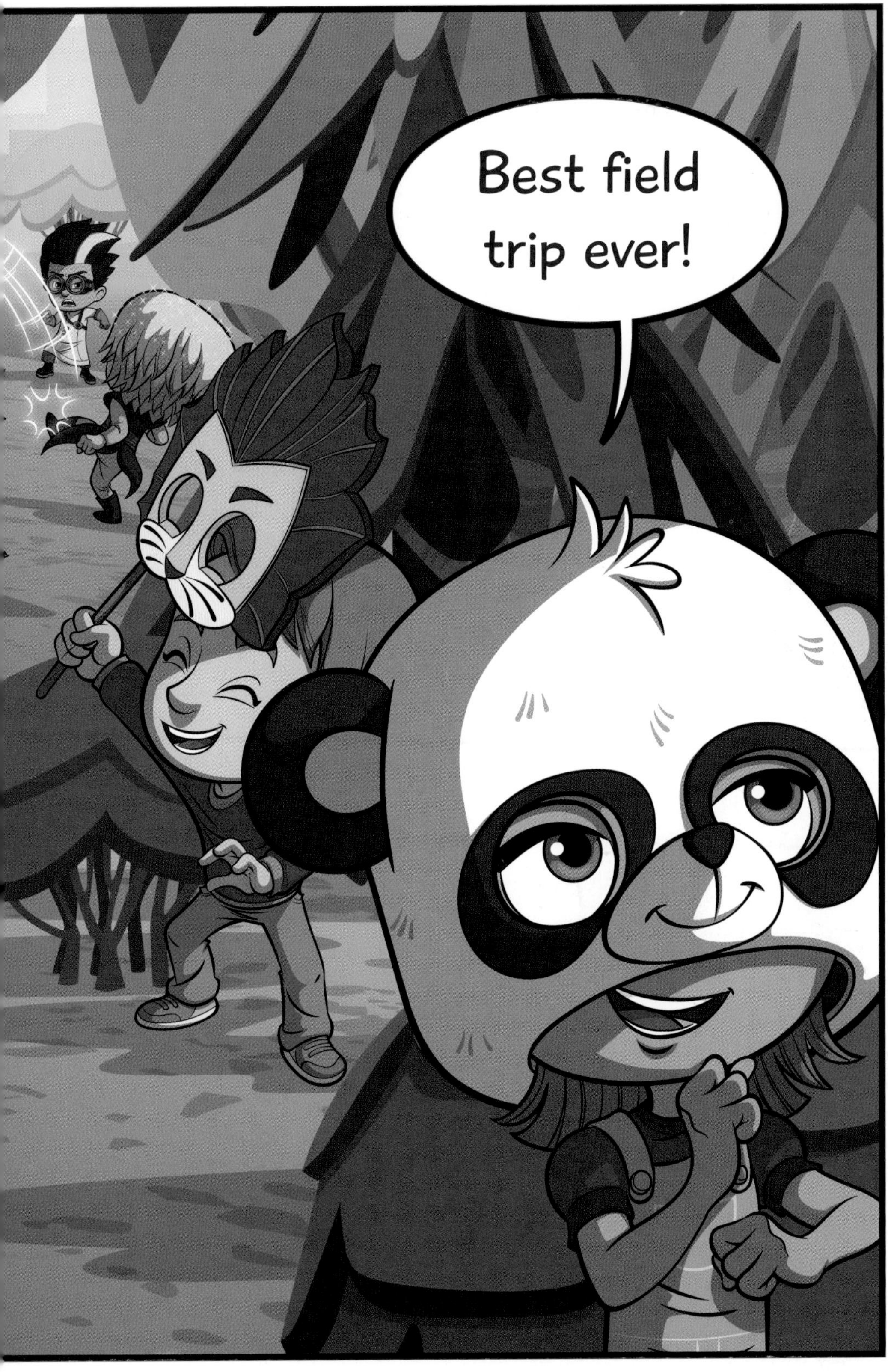
Best field trip ever!

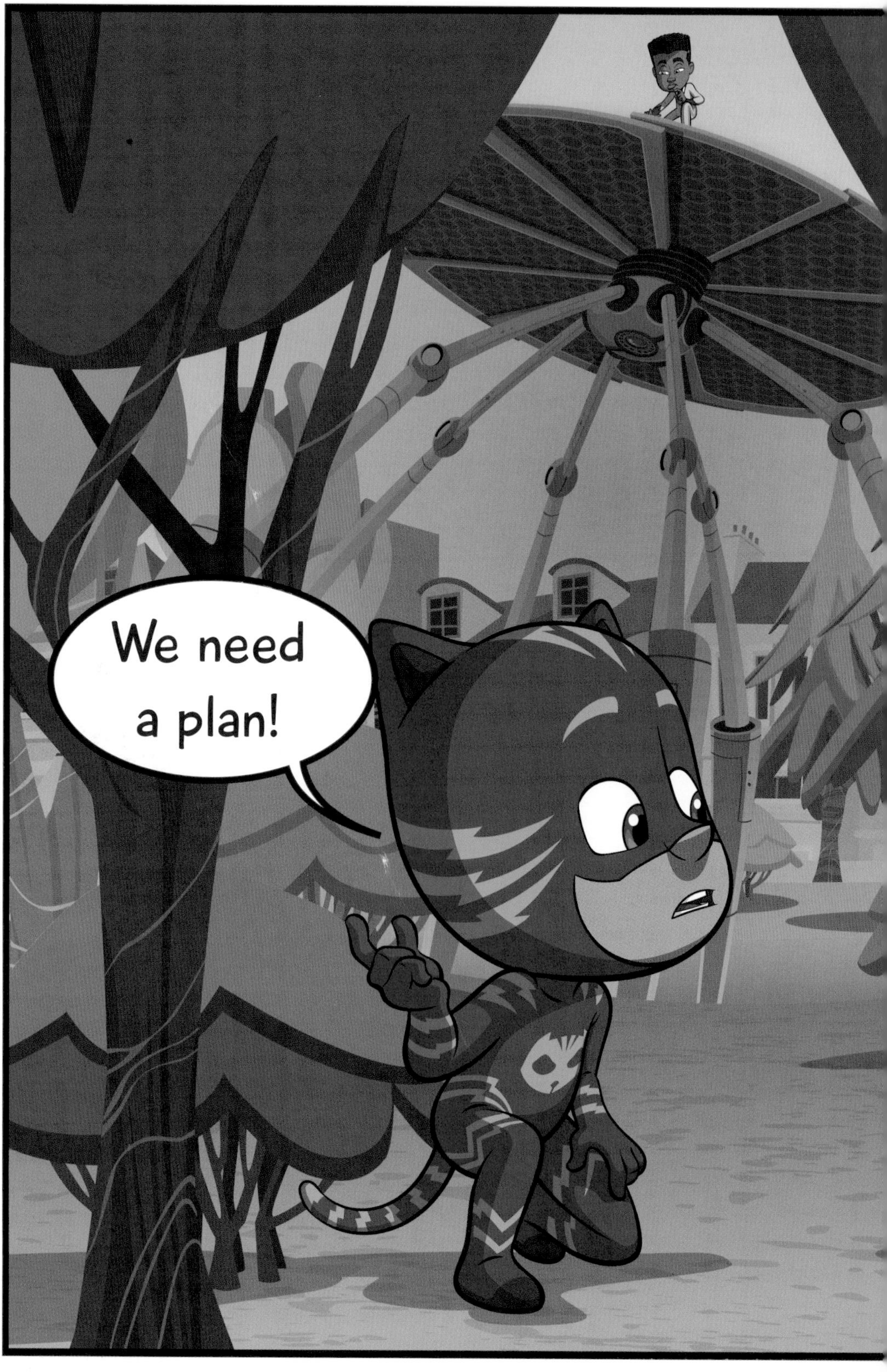
We need a plan!

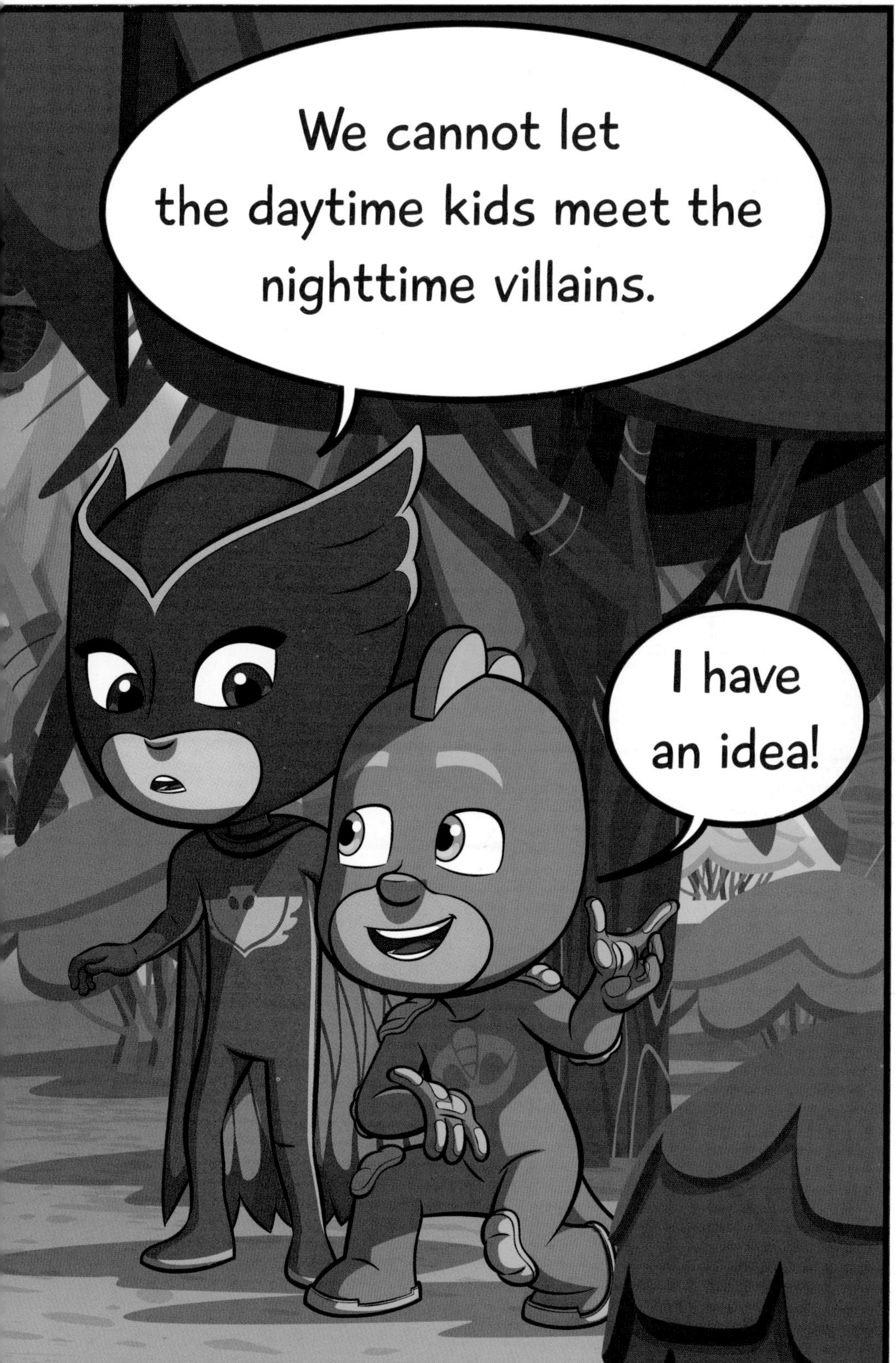
We cannot let the daytime kids meet the nighttime villains.
I have an idea!

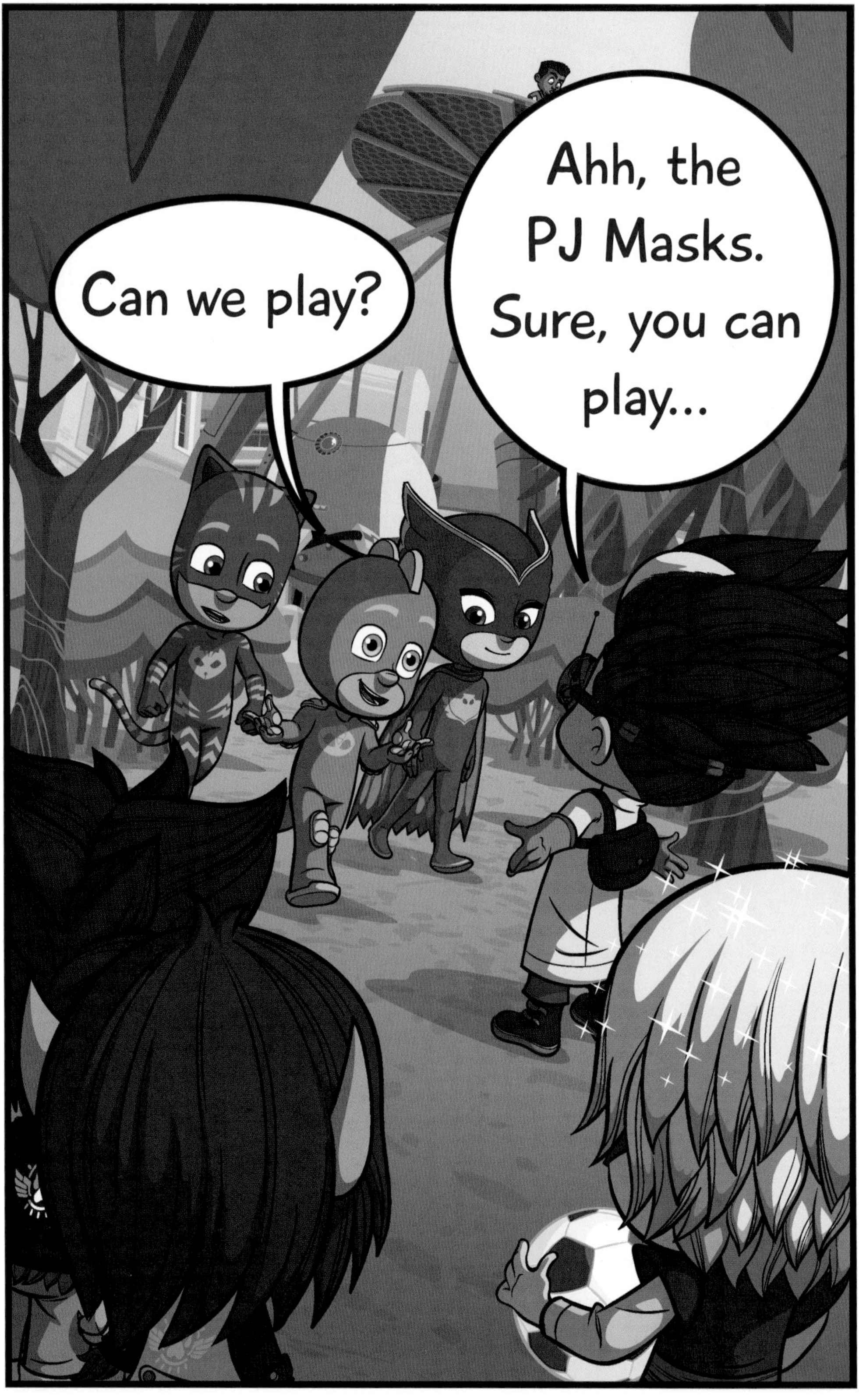
Can we play?
Ahh, the PJ Masks. Sure, you can play...

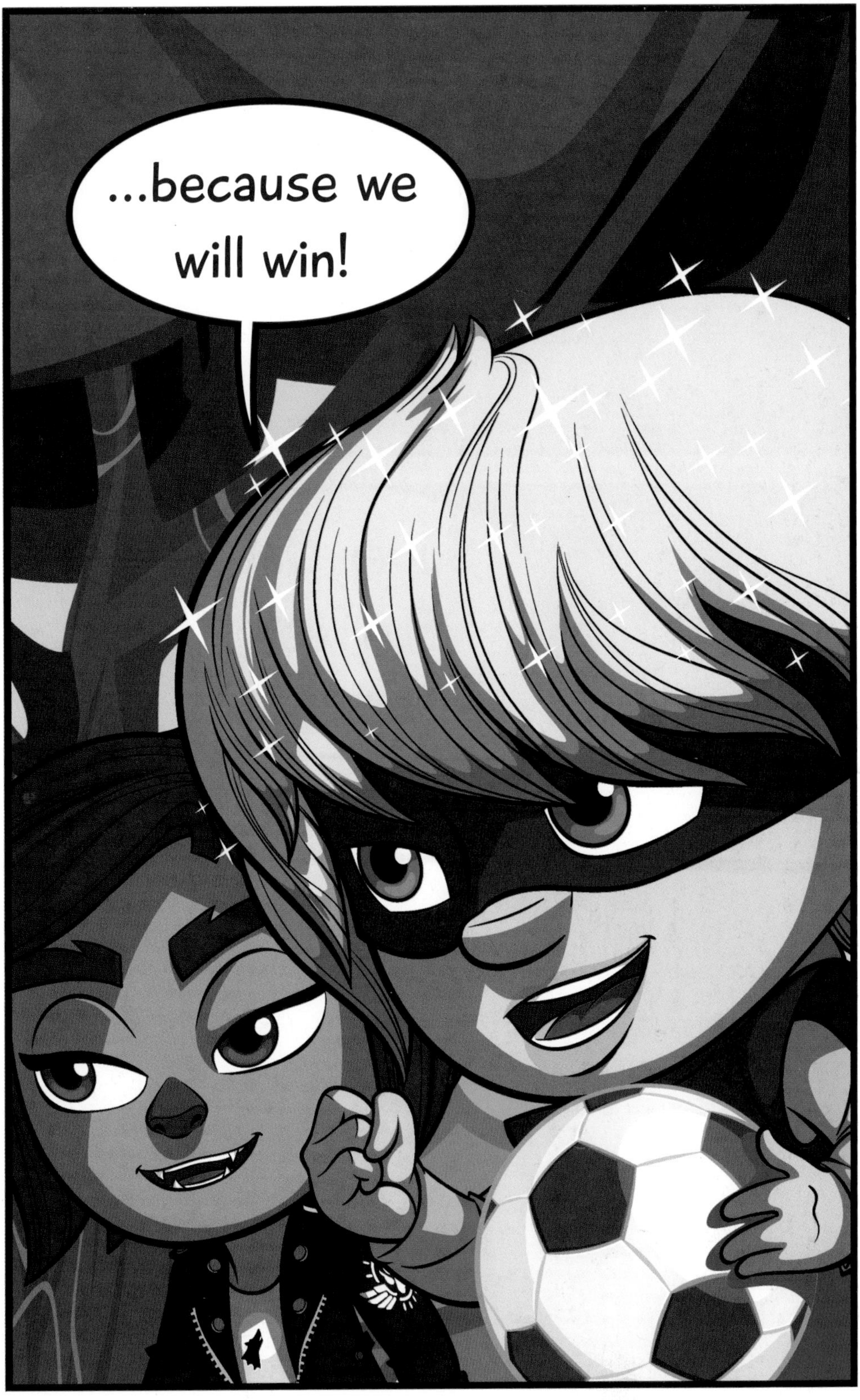
...because we will win!

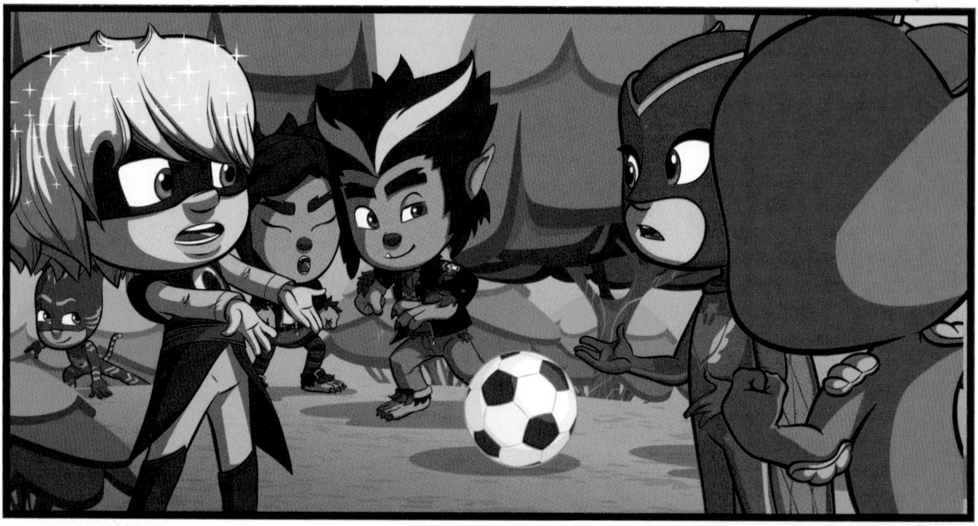

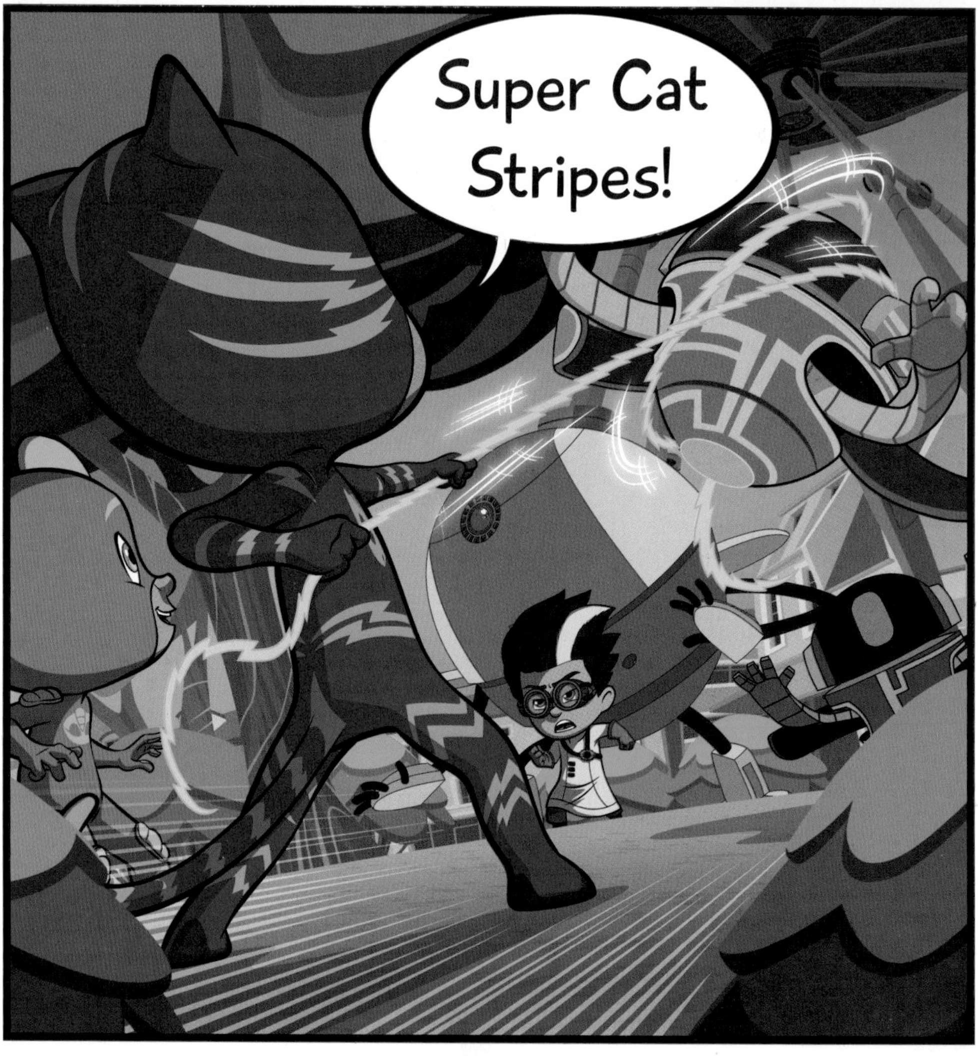
Super Cat Stripes!

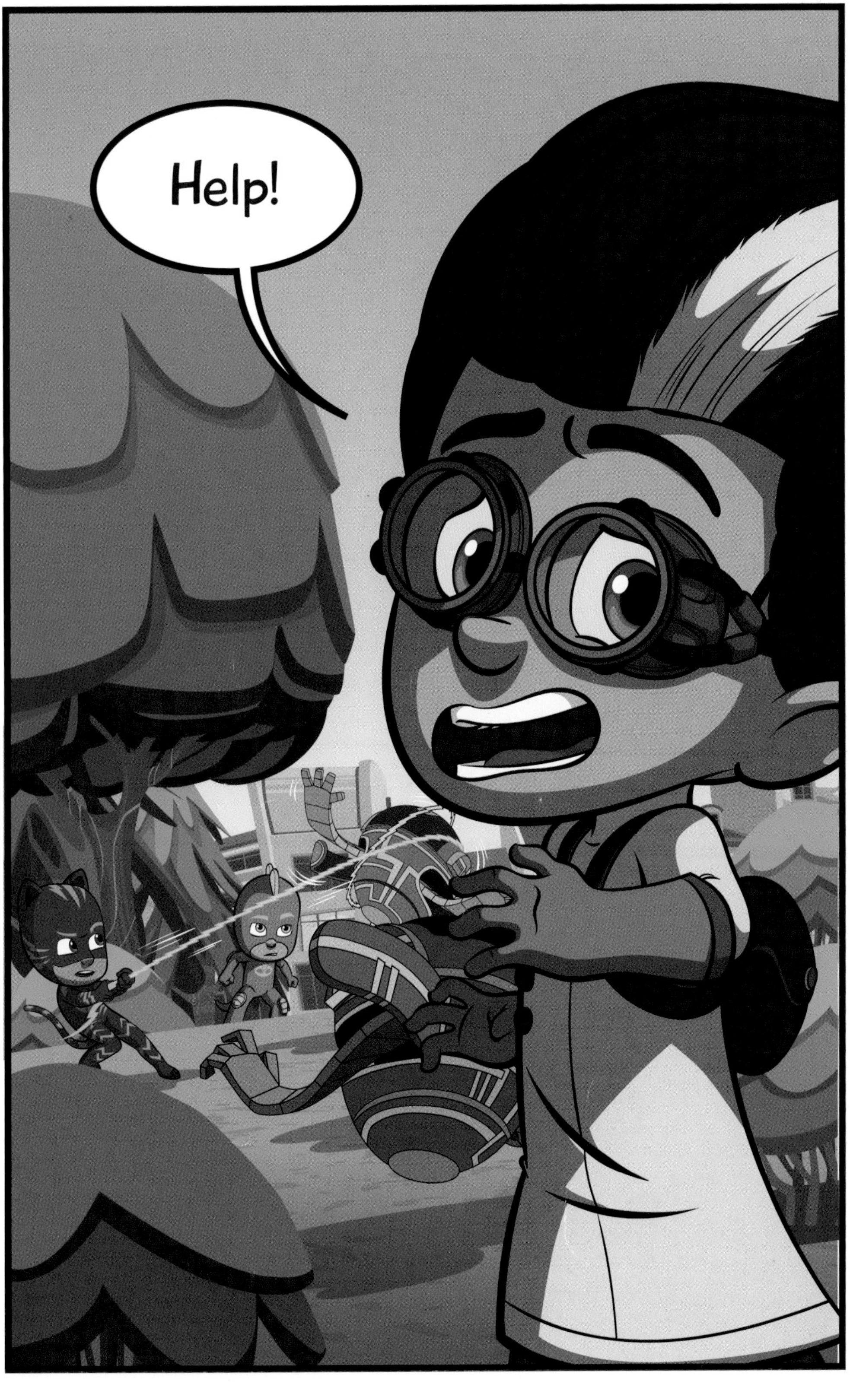
Help!

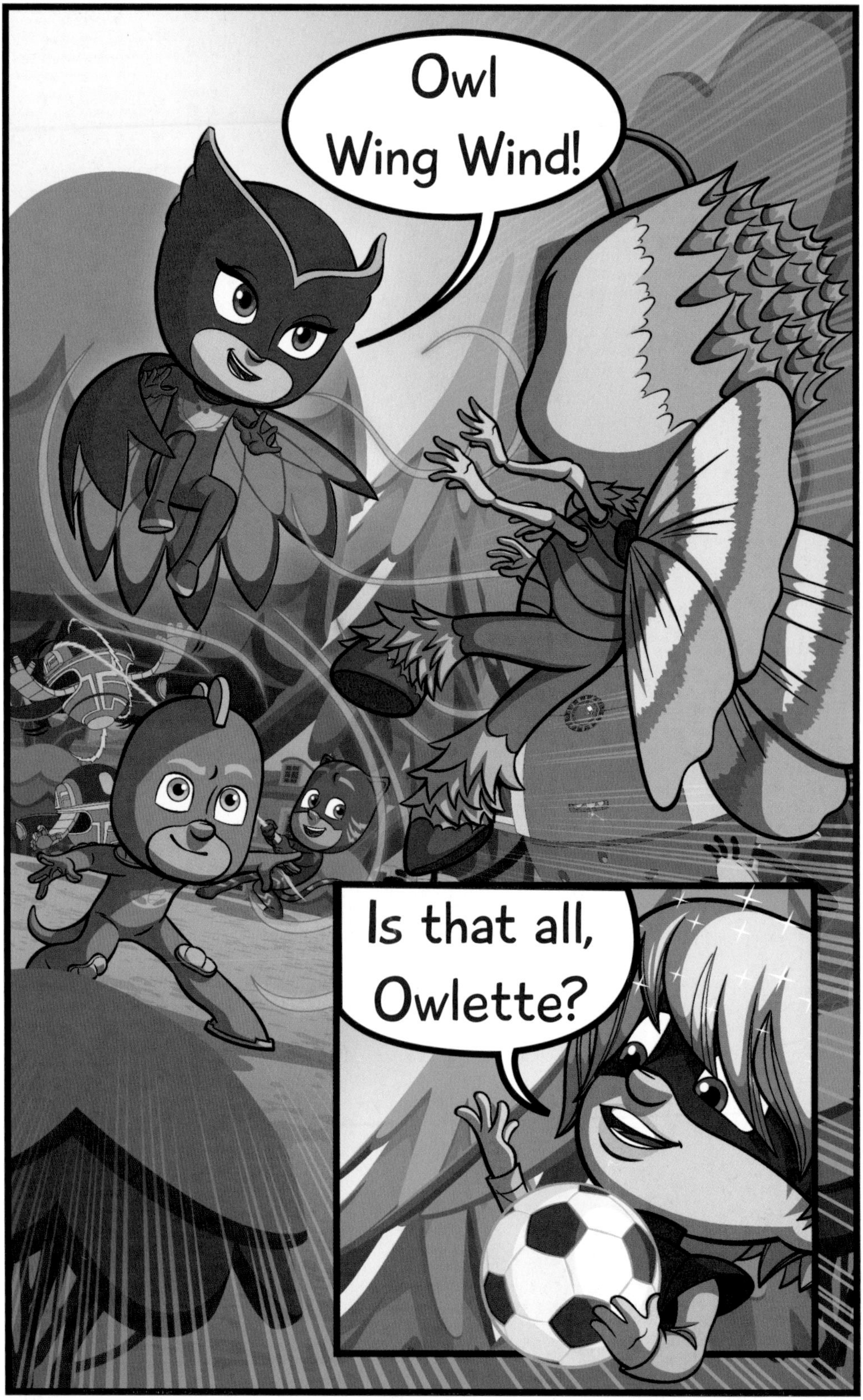
Owl Wing Wind!
Is that all, Owlette?

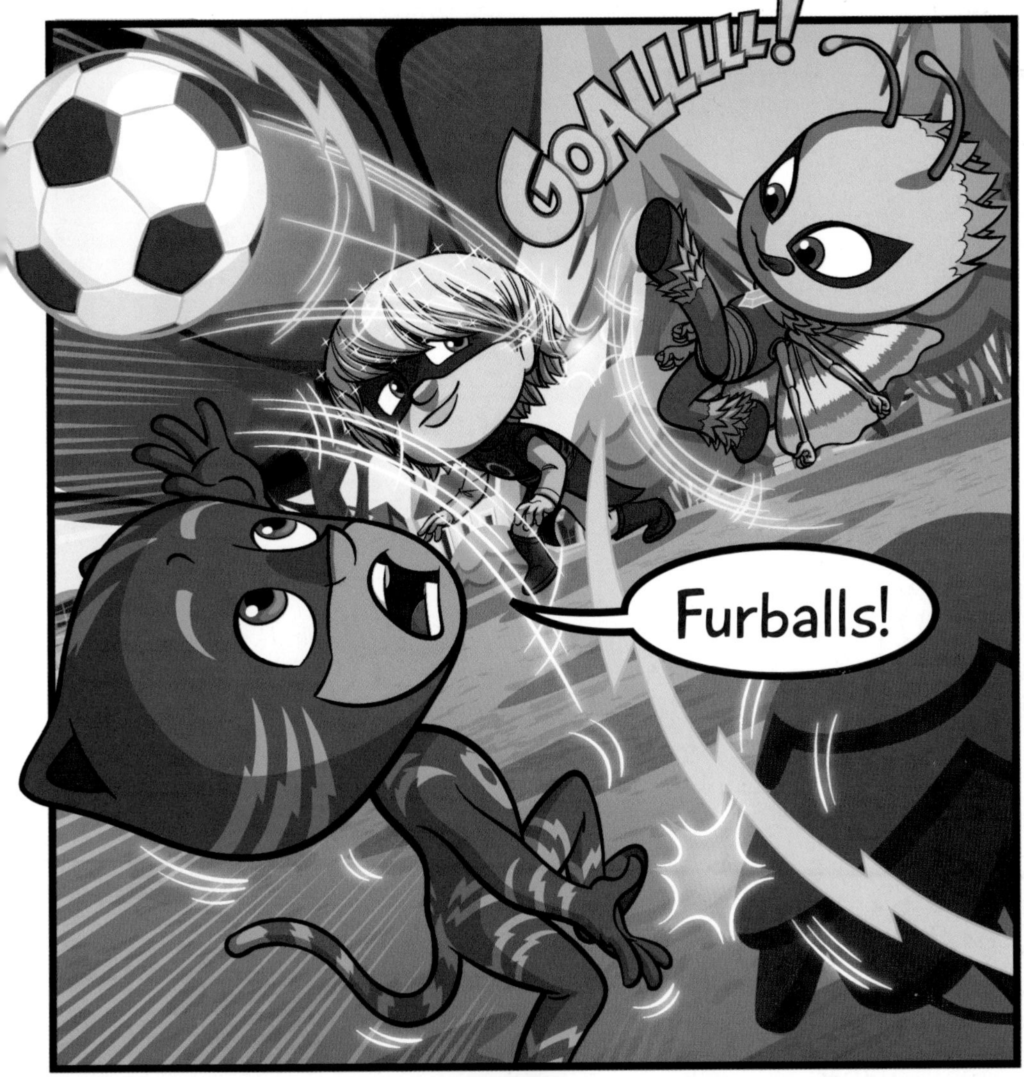
GOALLLLL!
Furballs!

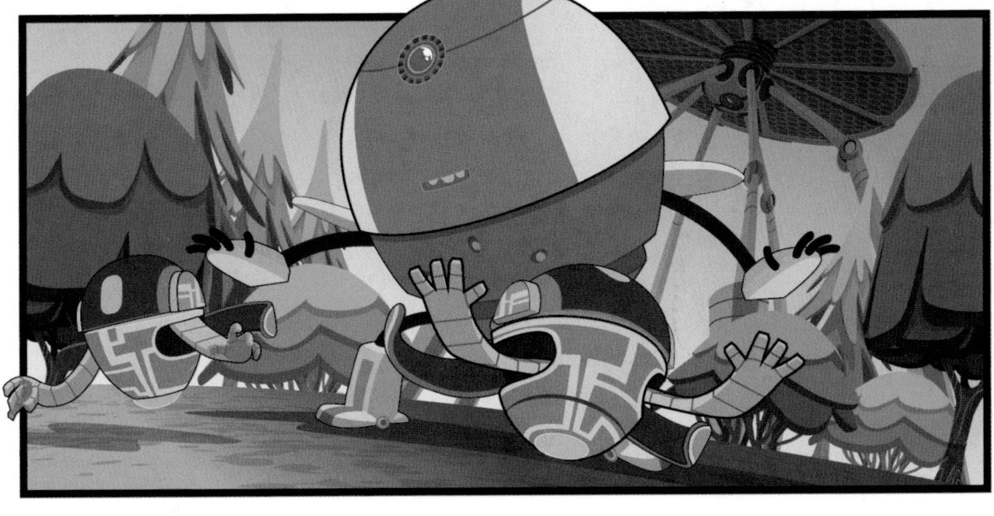

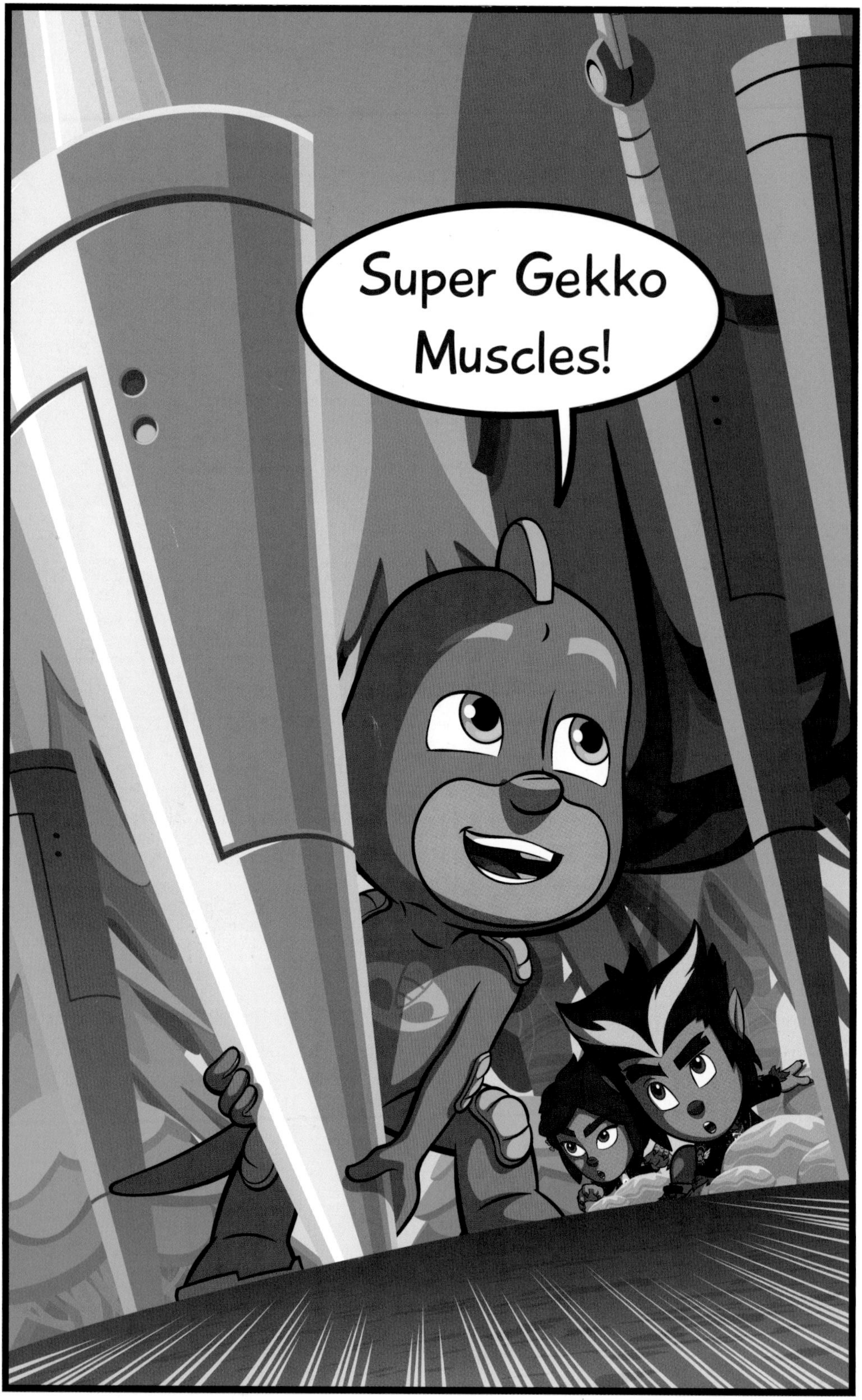
Super Gekko Muscles!

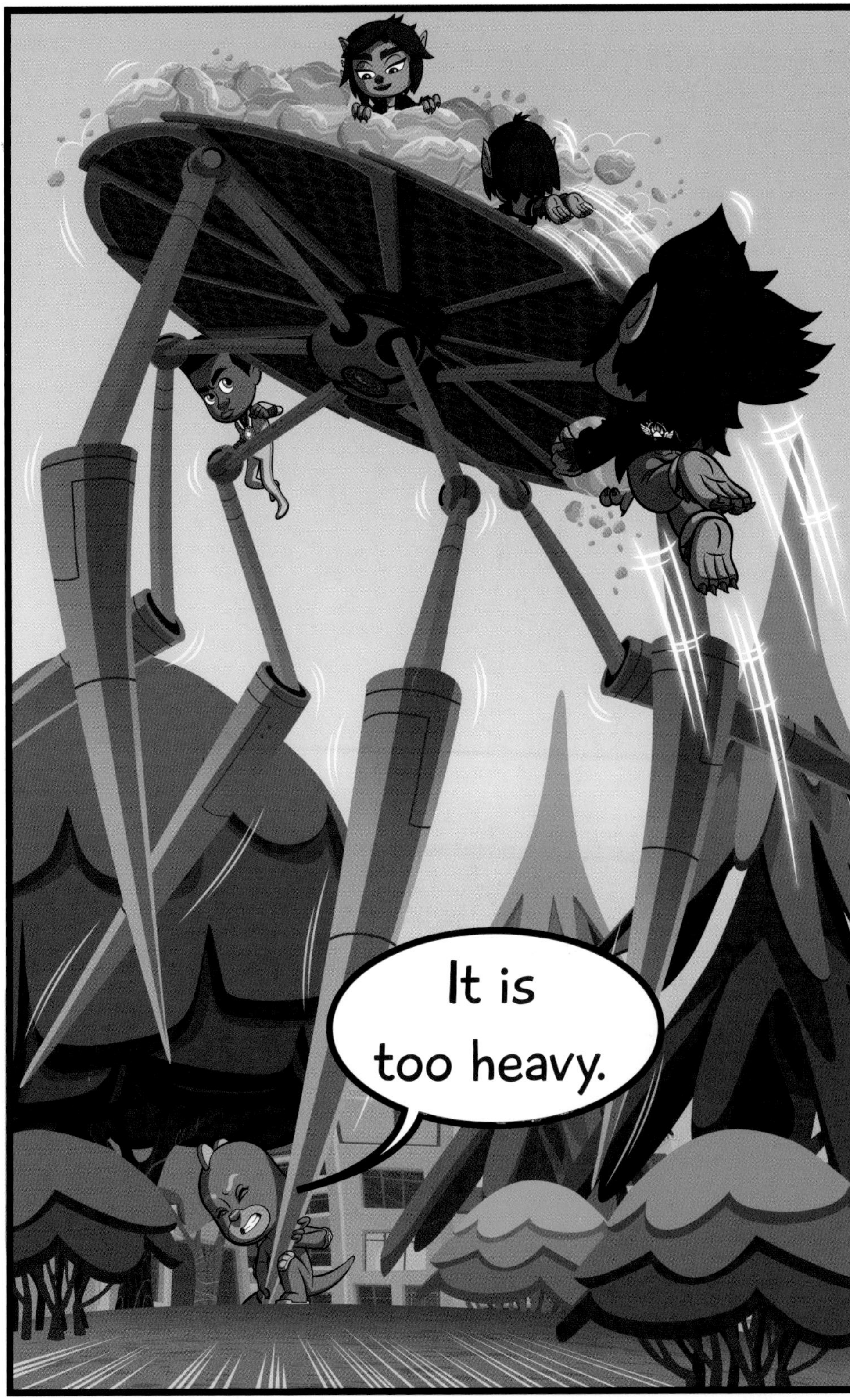
It is too heavy.

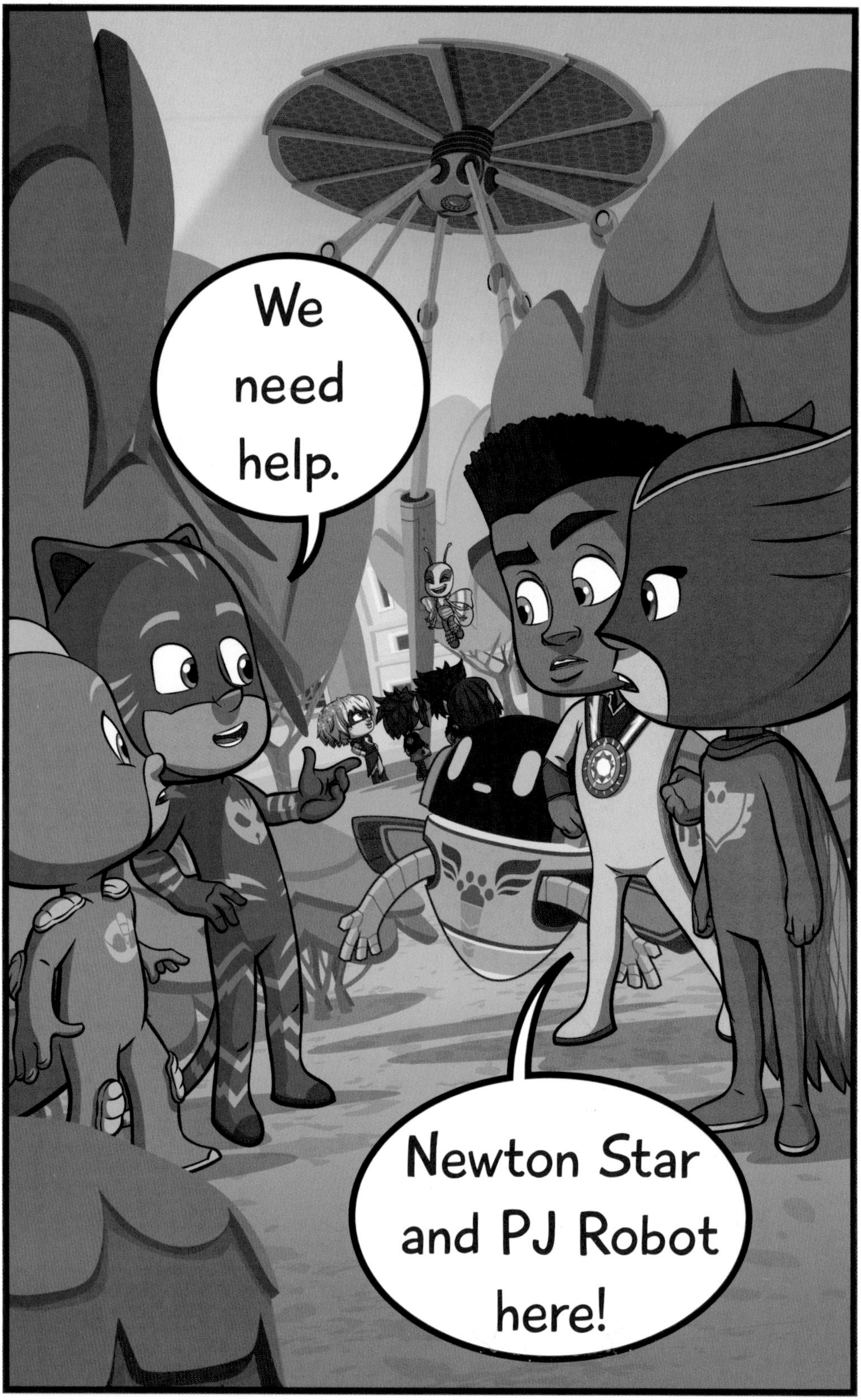
We need help.
Newton Star and PJ Robot here!

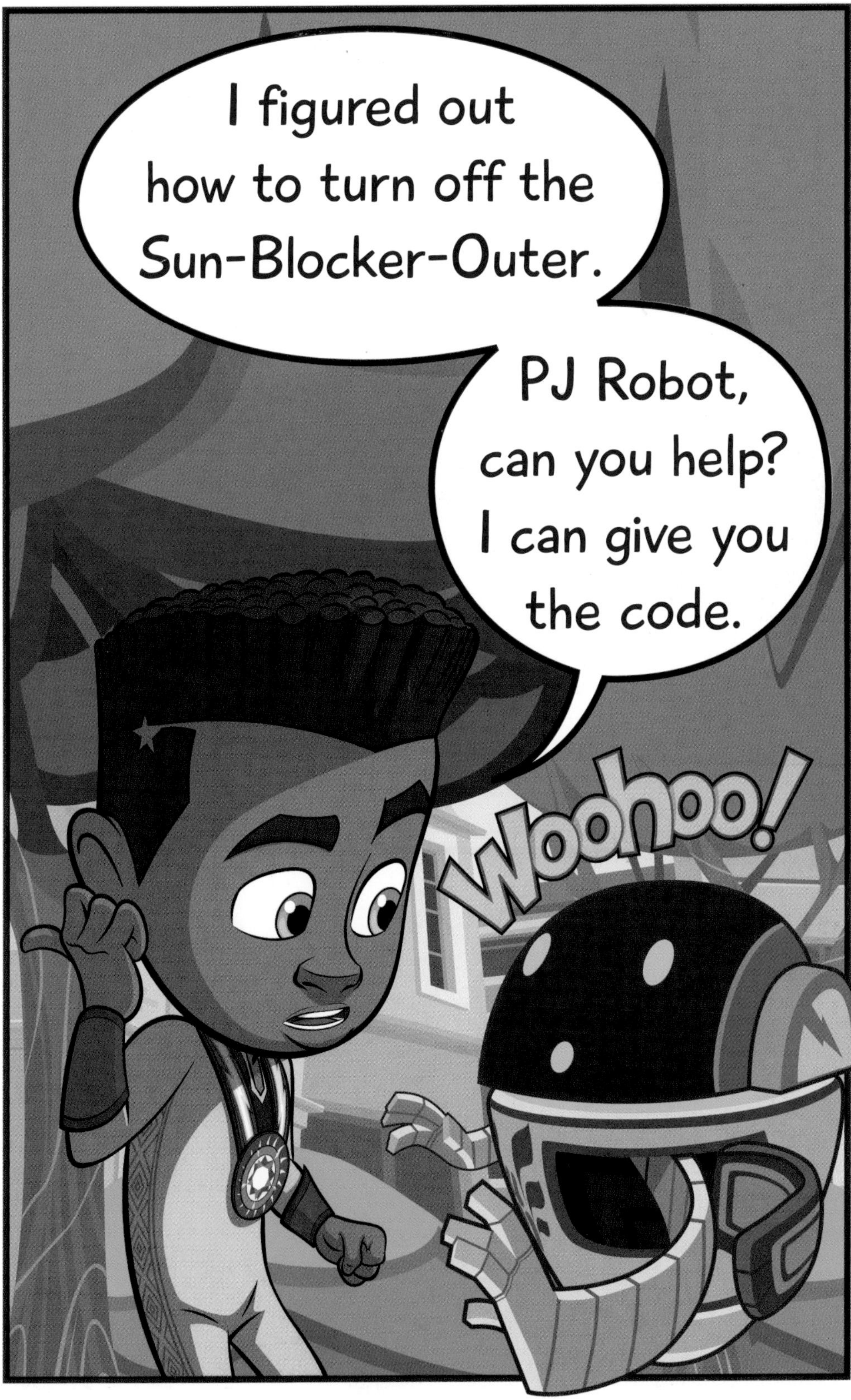
I figured out how to turn off the Sun-Blocker-Outer.
PJ Robot, can you help? I can give you the code.
Woohoo!

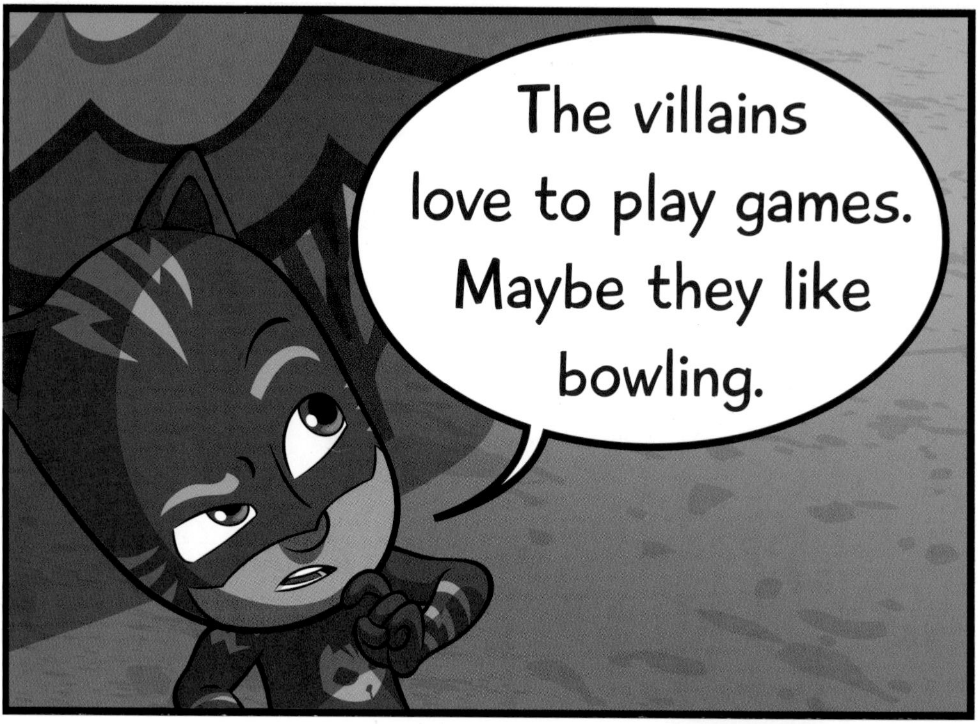
The villains love to play games. Maybe they like bowling.

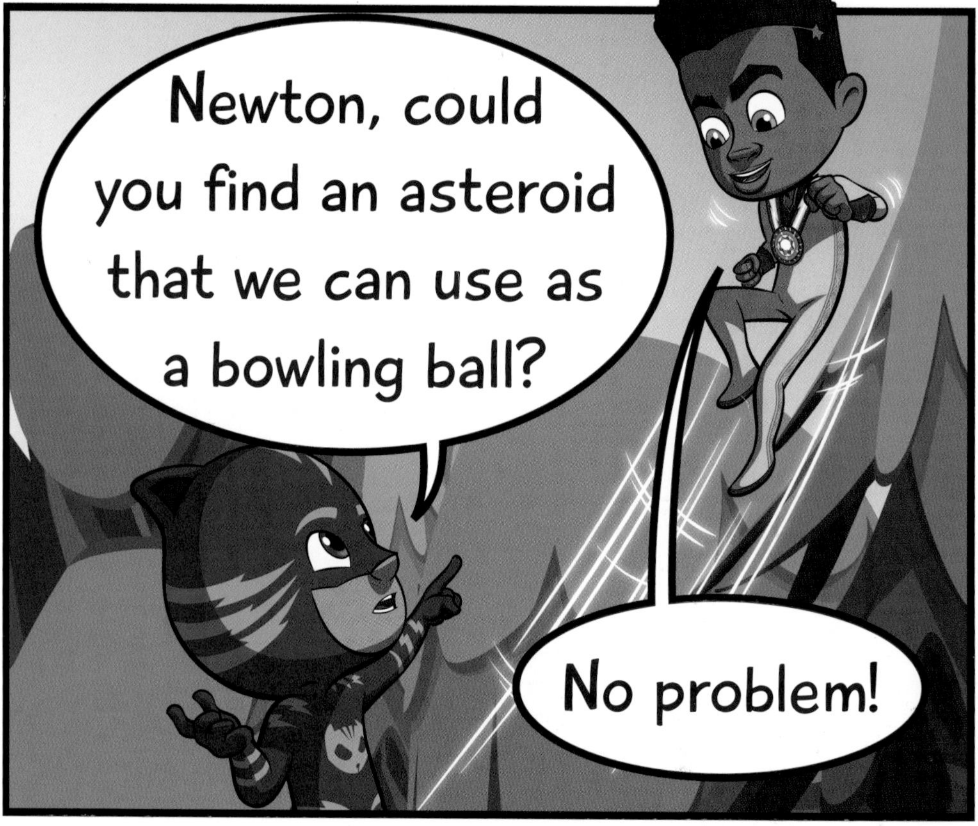
Newton, could you find an asteroid that we can use as a bowling ball?
No problem!

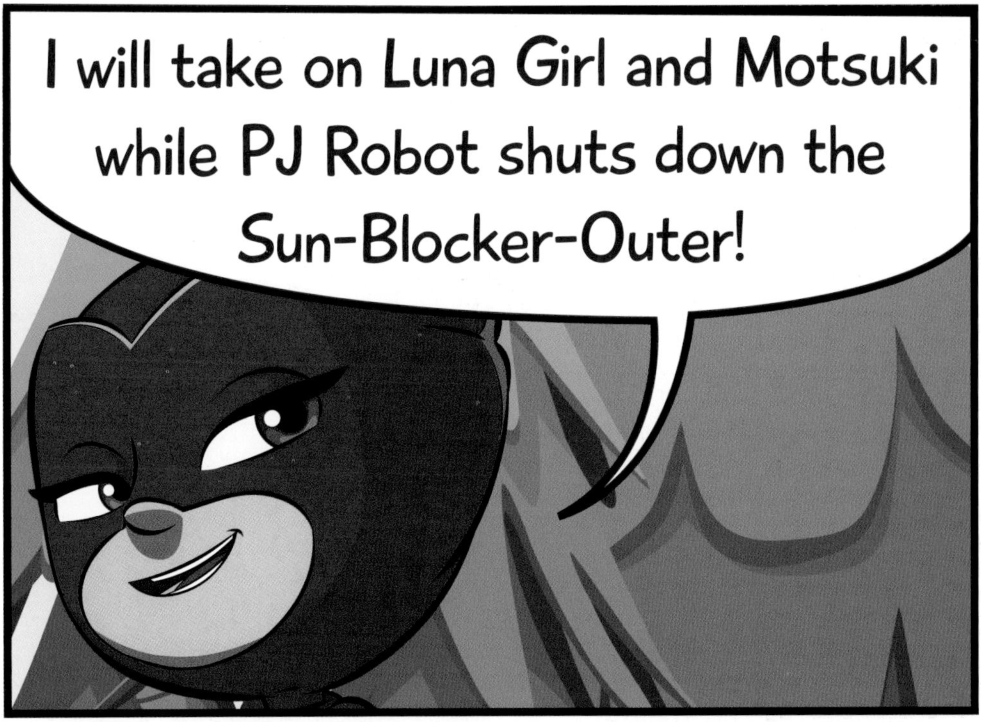
I will take on Luna Girl and Motsuki while PJ Robot shuts down the Sun-Blocker-Outer!

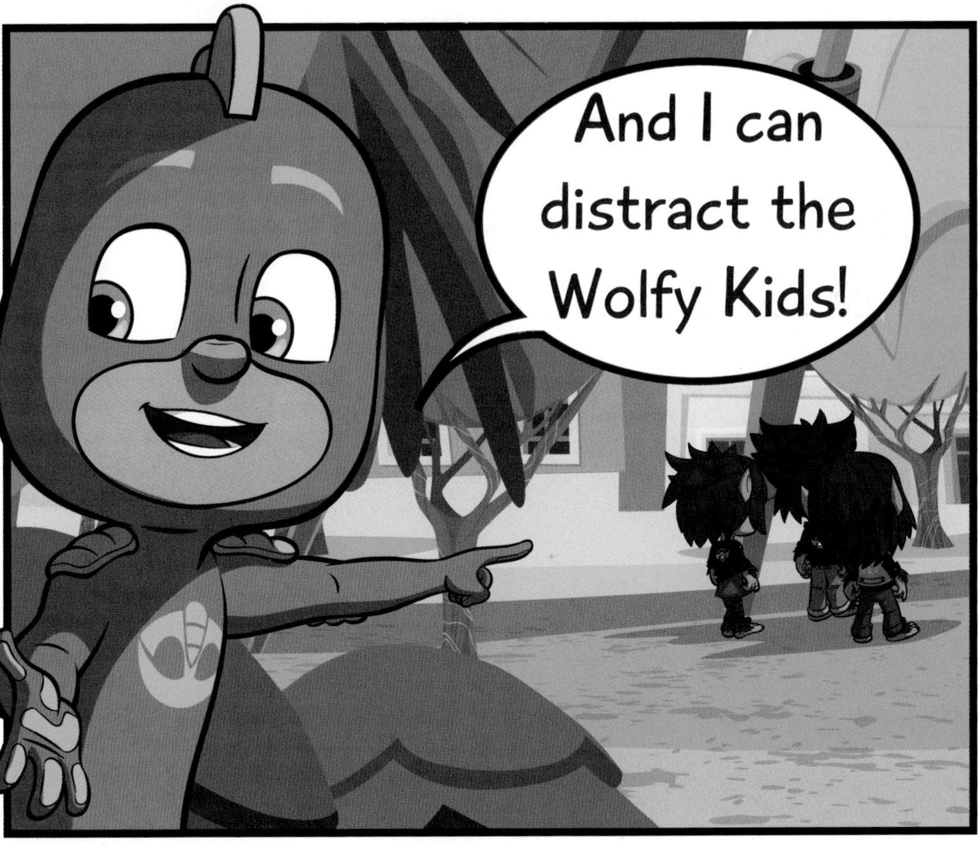
And I can distract the Wolfy Kids!

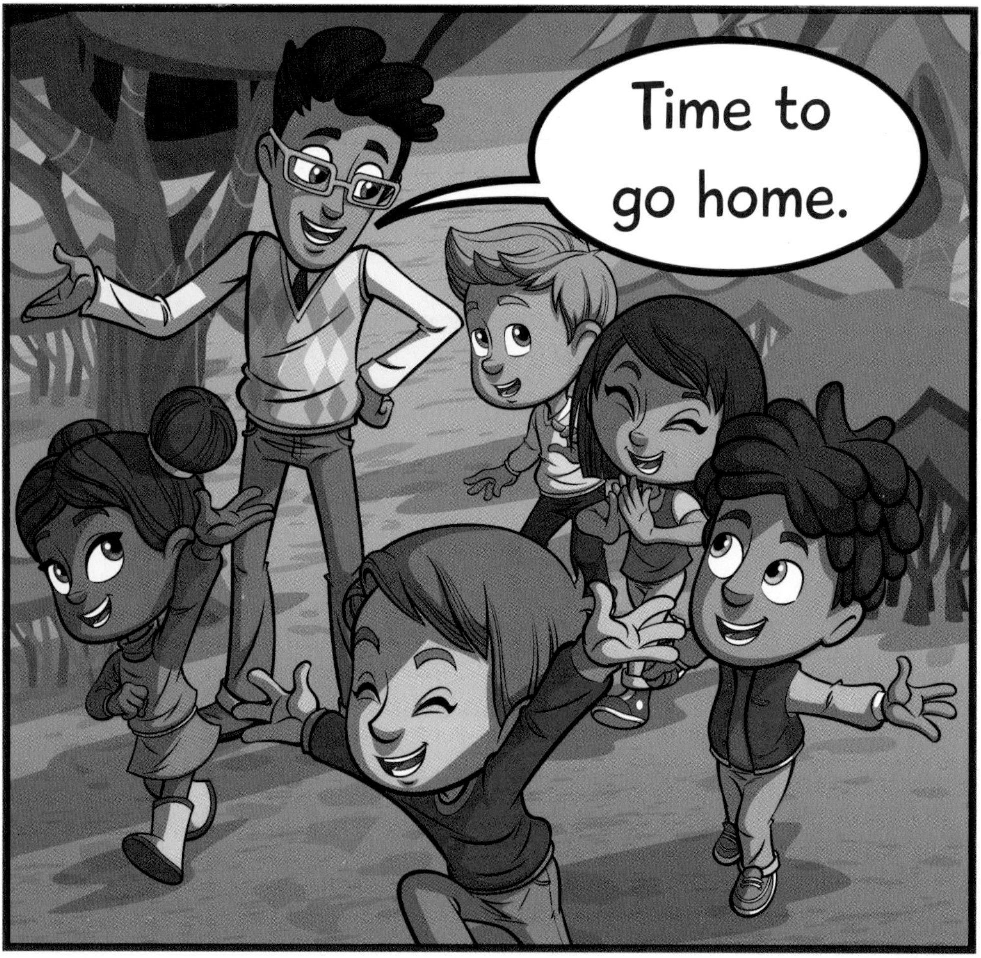
Time to go home.

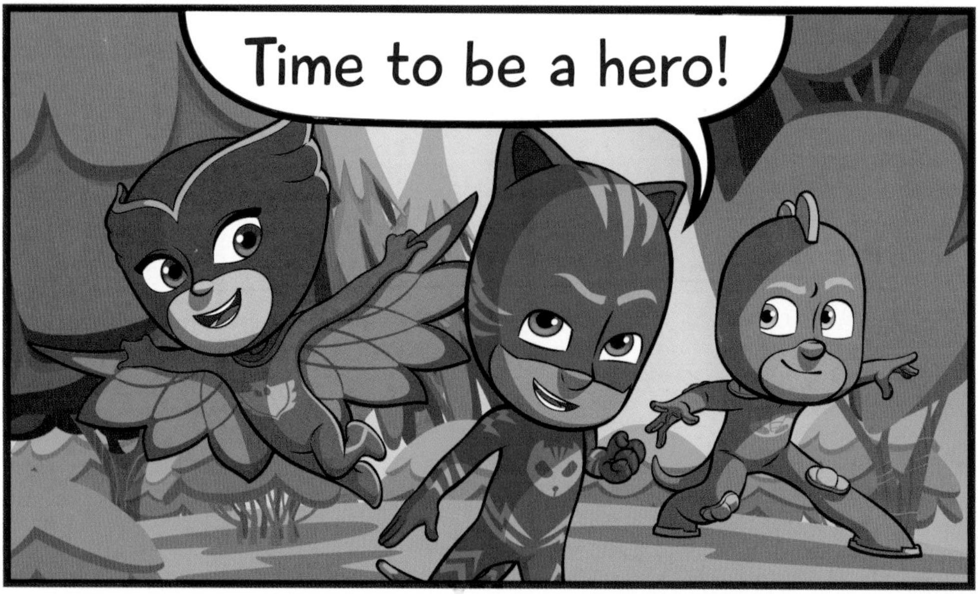
Time to be a hero!

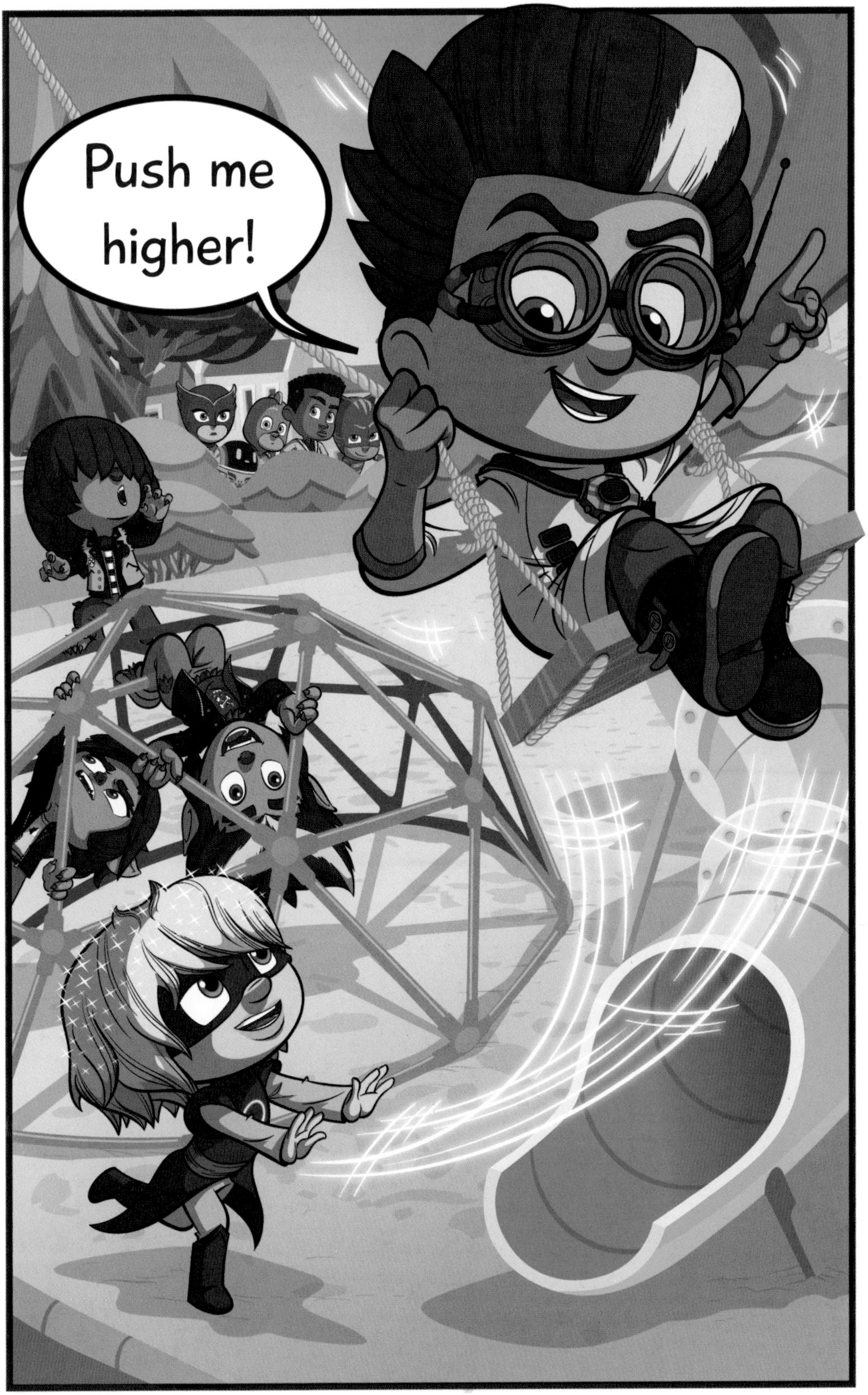
Push me higher!

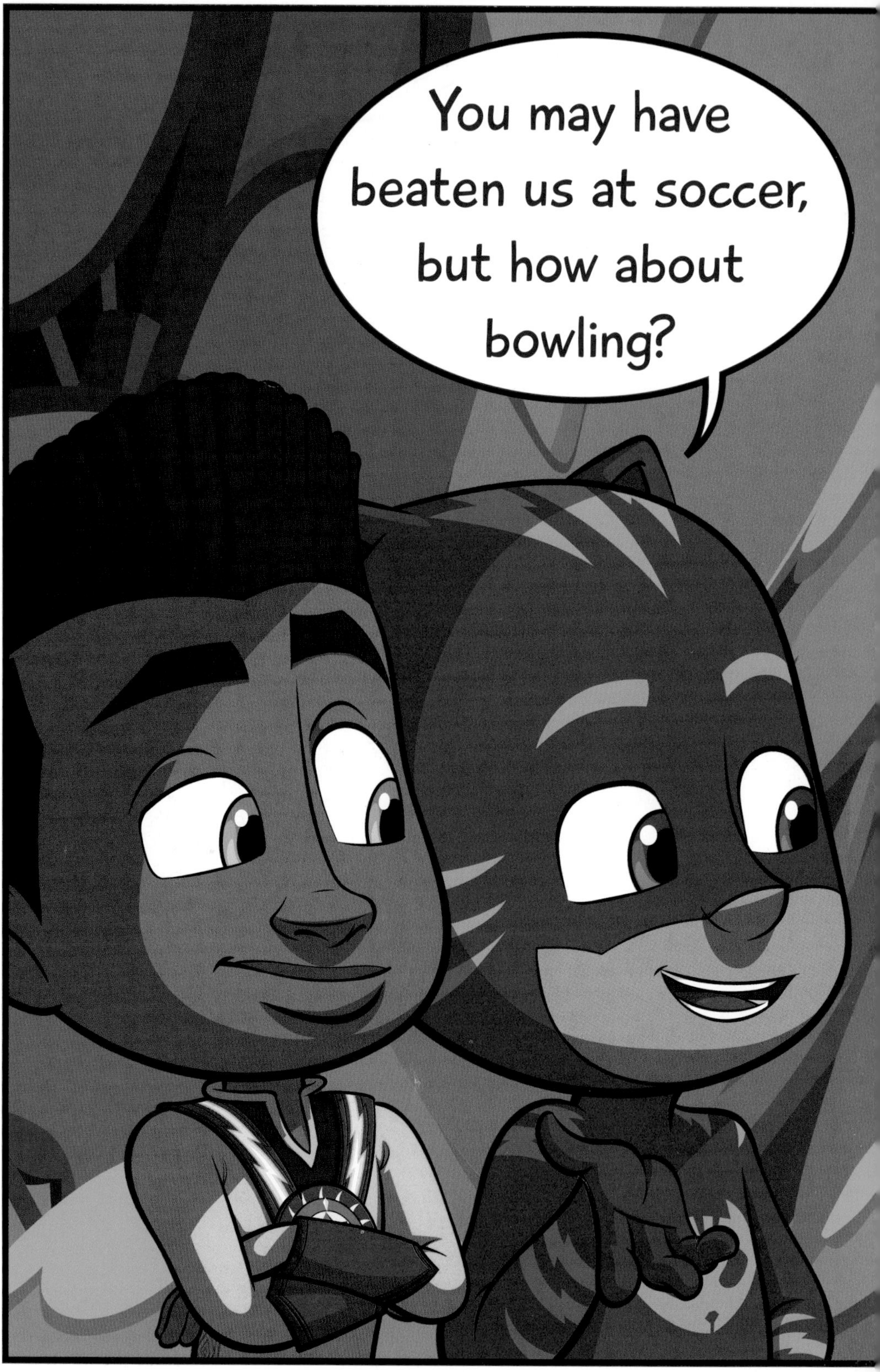
You may have beaten us at *soccer*, but how about bowling?

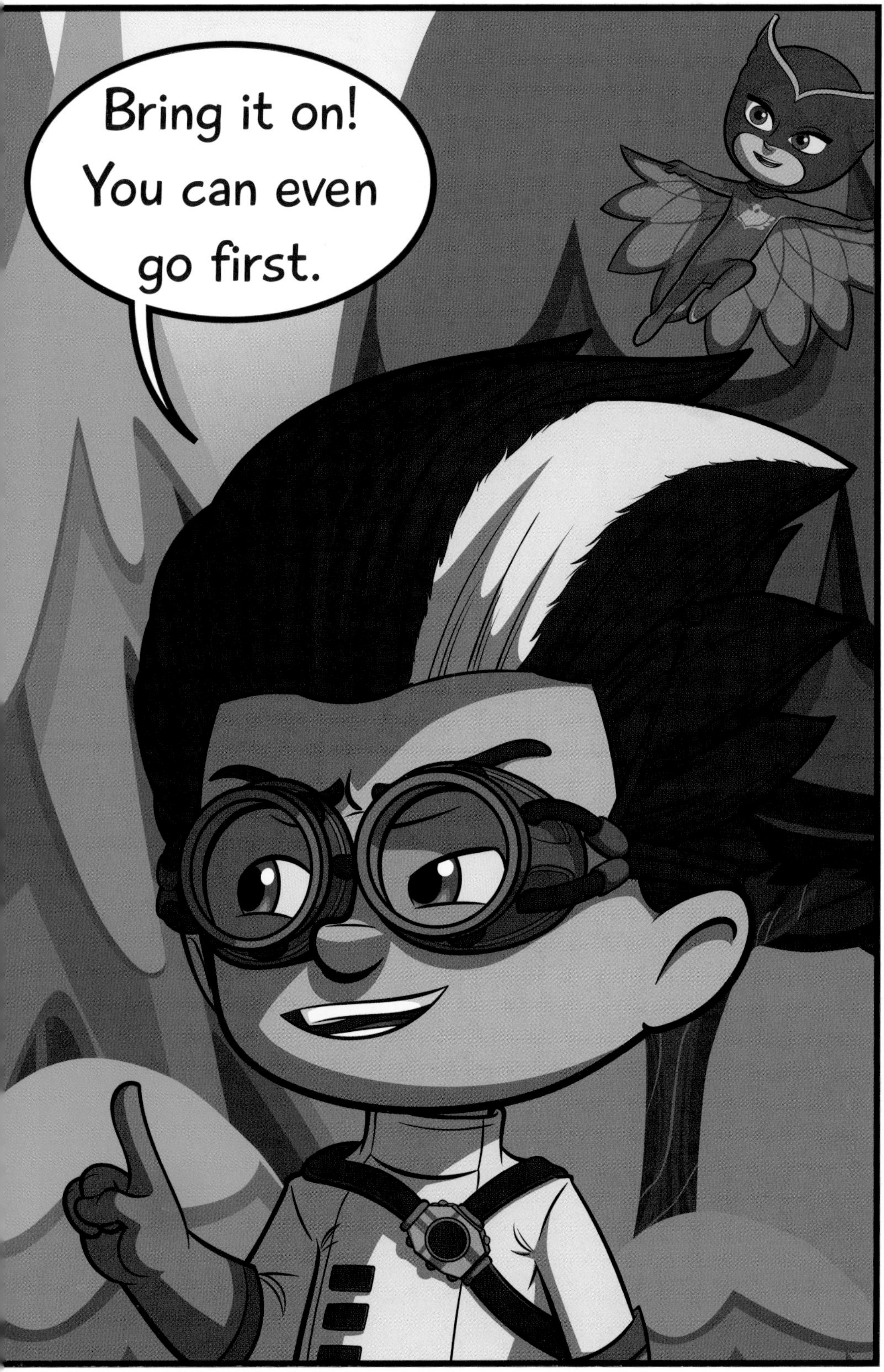
Bring it on! You can even go first.

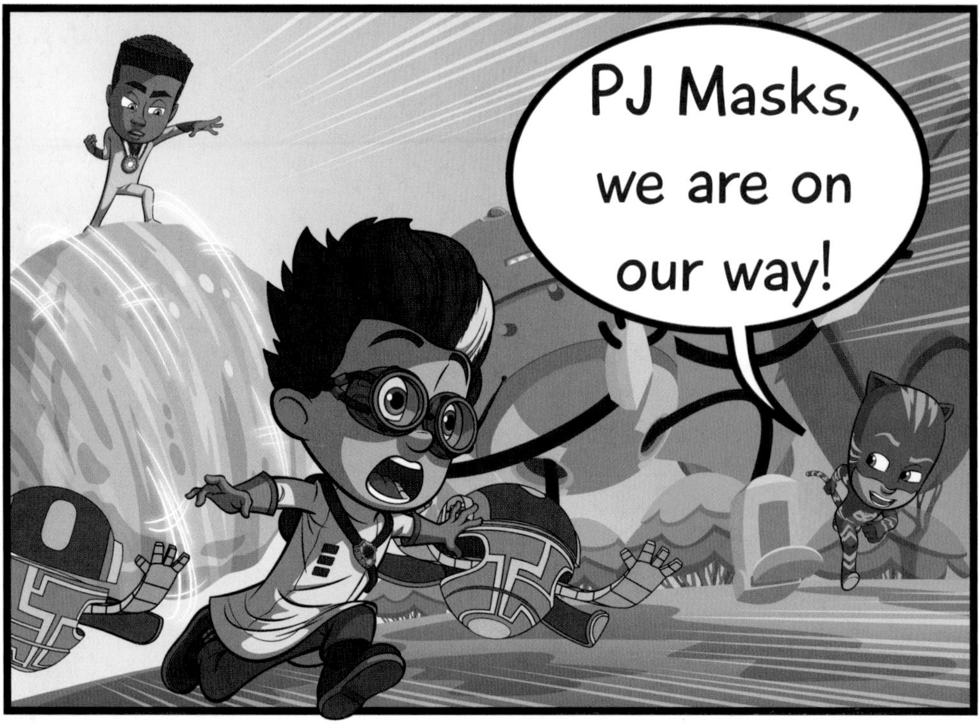
PJ Masks,
we are on
our way!

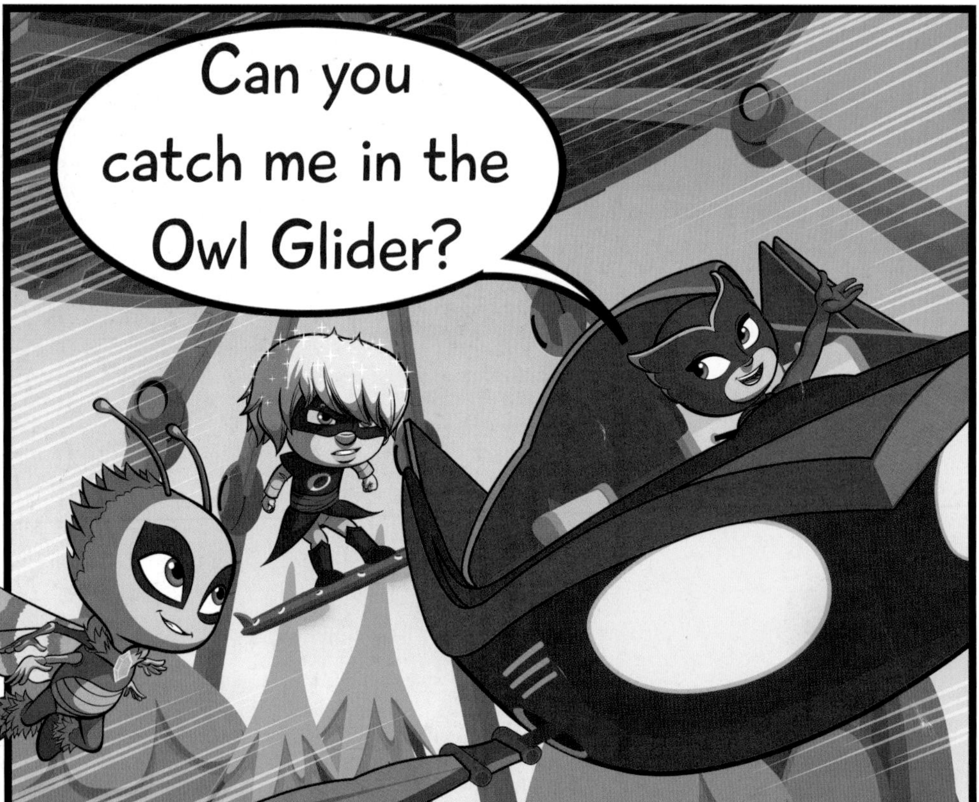
Can you
catch me in the
Owl Glider?

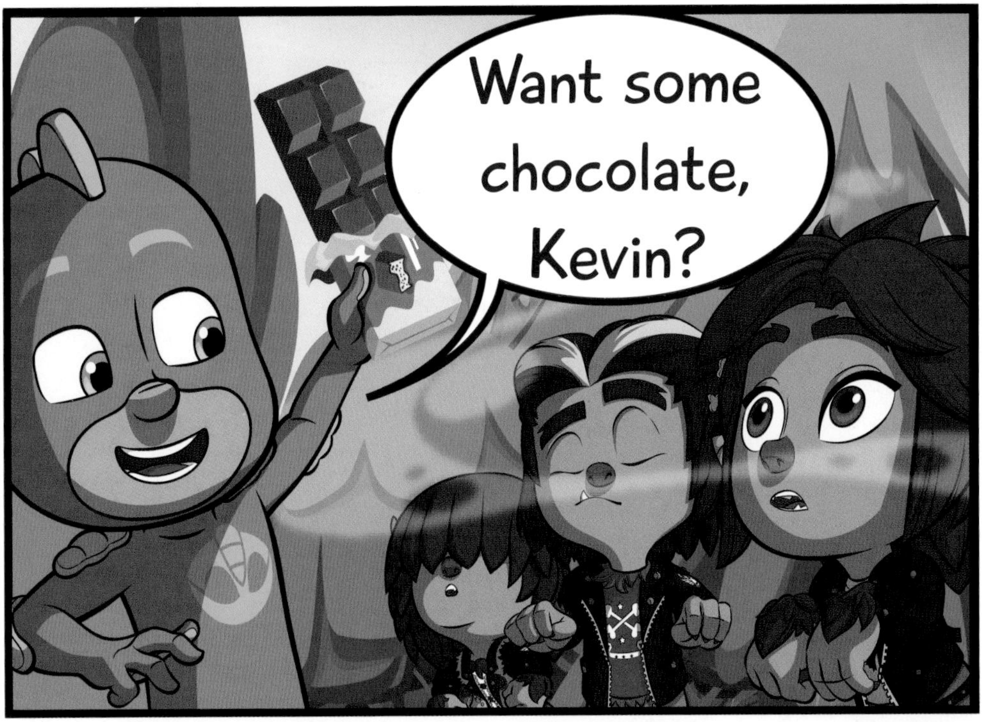
Want some chocolate, Kevin?

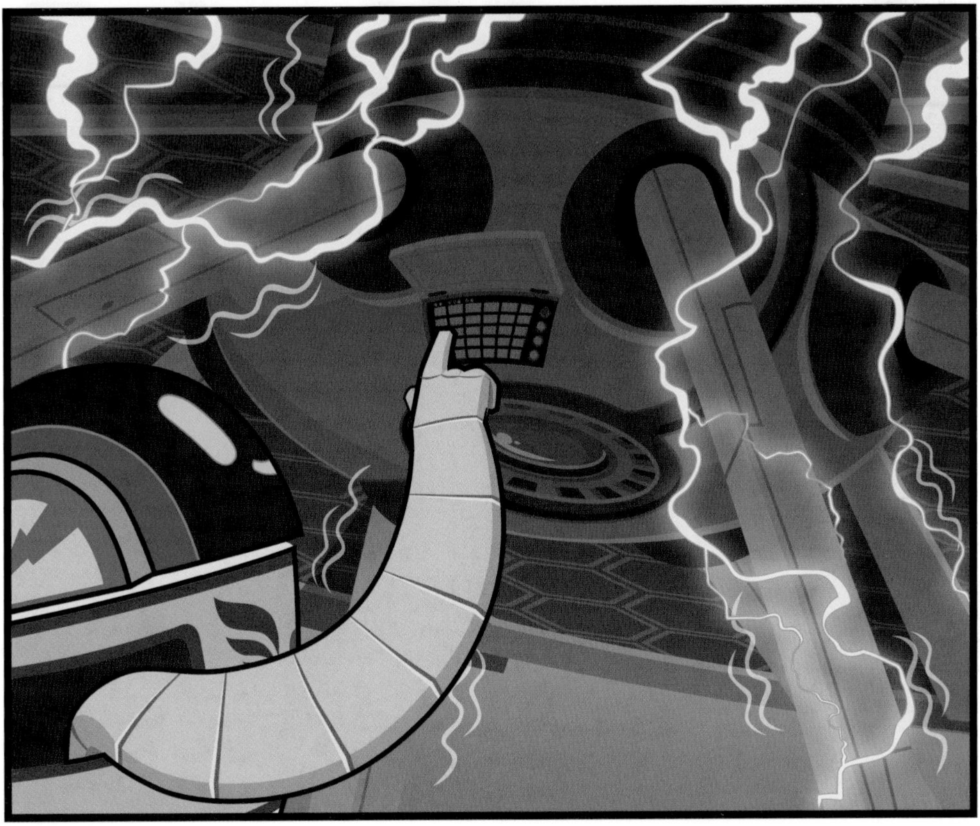

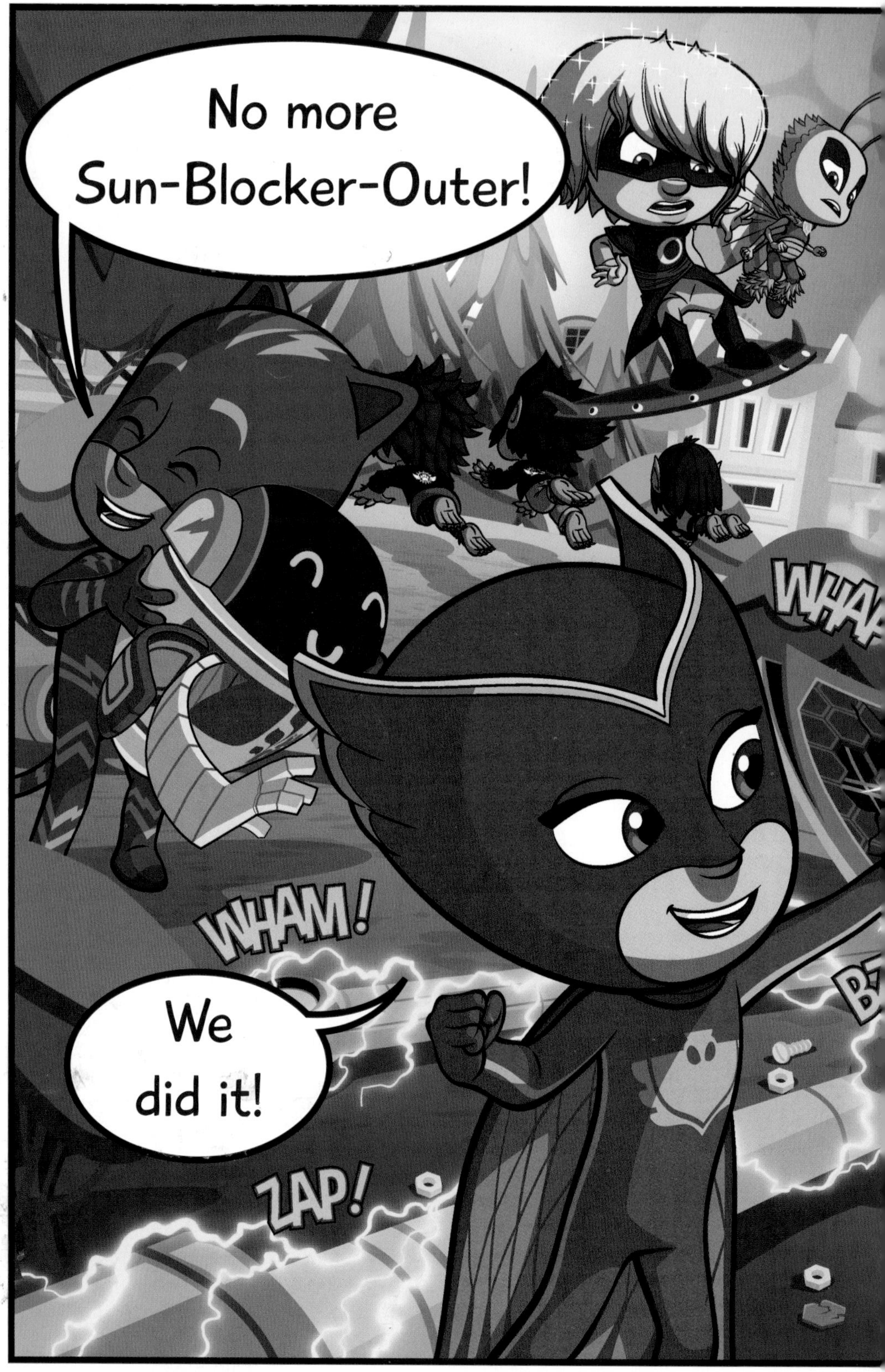
No more Sun-Blocker-Outer!
WHAM!
WHAM!
We did it!
ZAP!

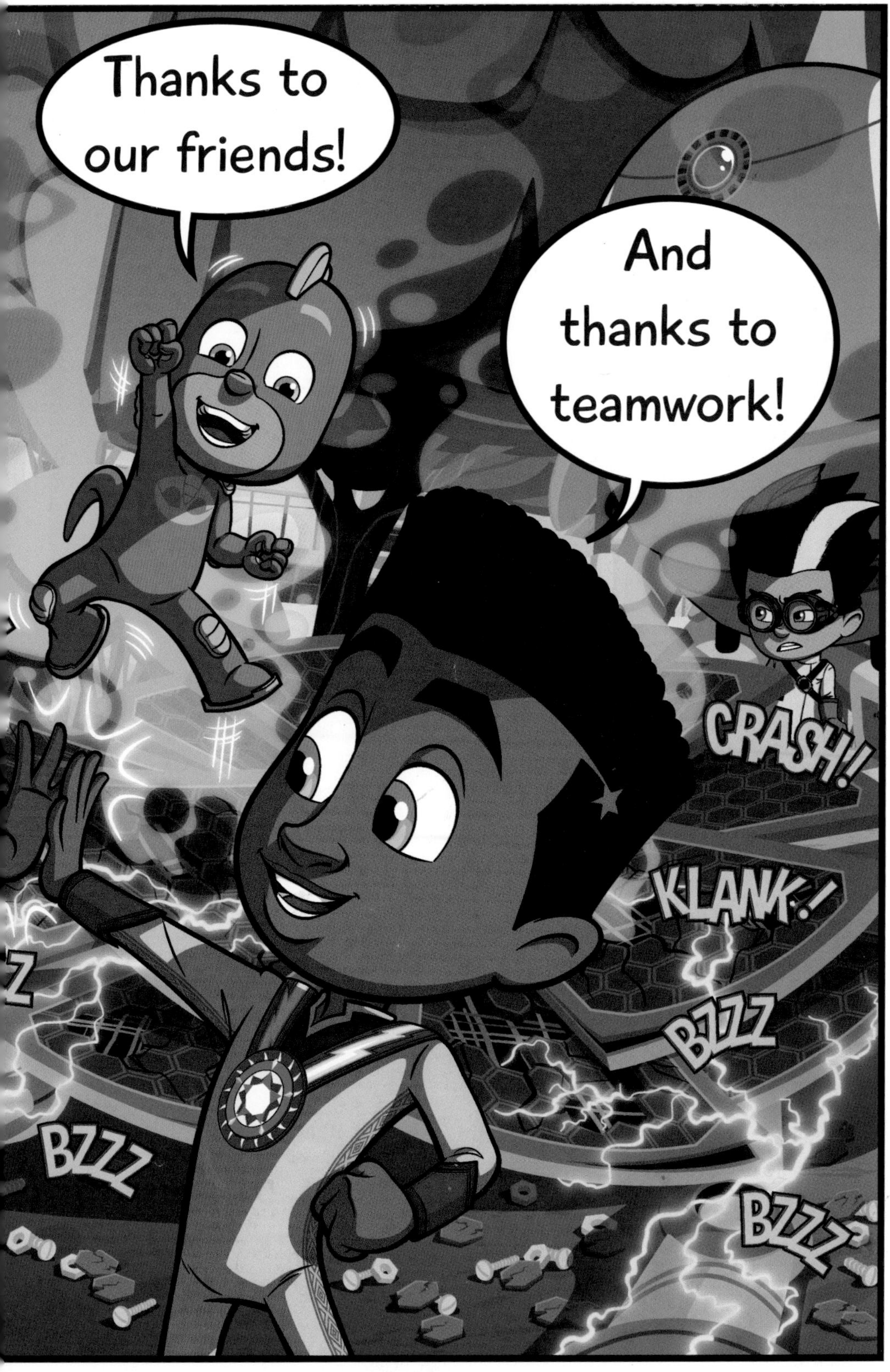
Thanks to our friends!
And thanks to teamwork!
CRASH!
KLANK!
BZZZ
BZZZ
BZZZ

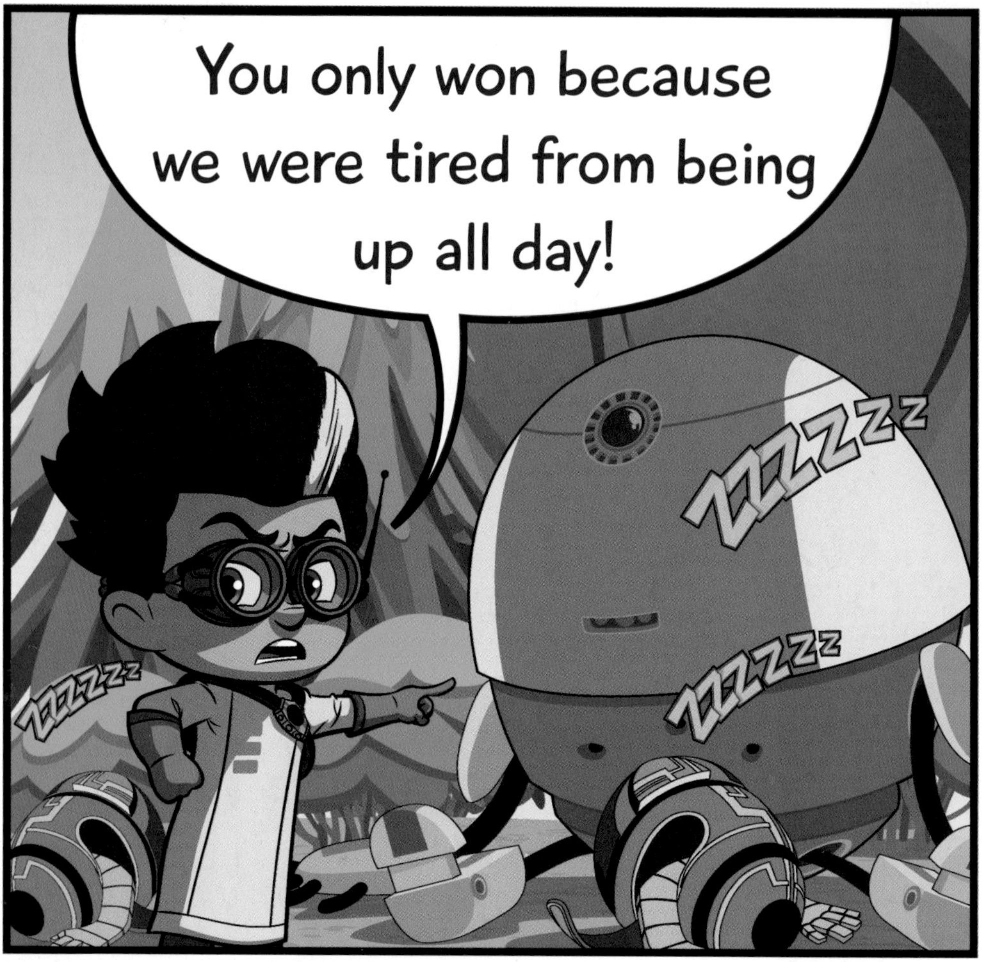
You only won because we were tired from being up all day!
ZZZZZZZ
ZZZZZZ
ZZZZZZ

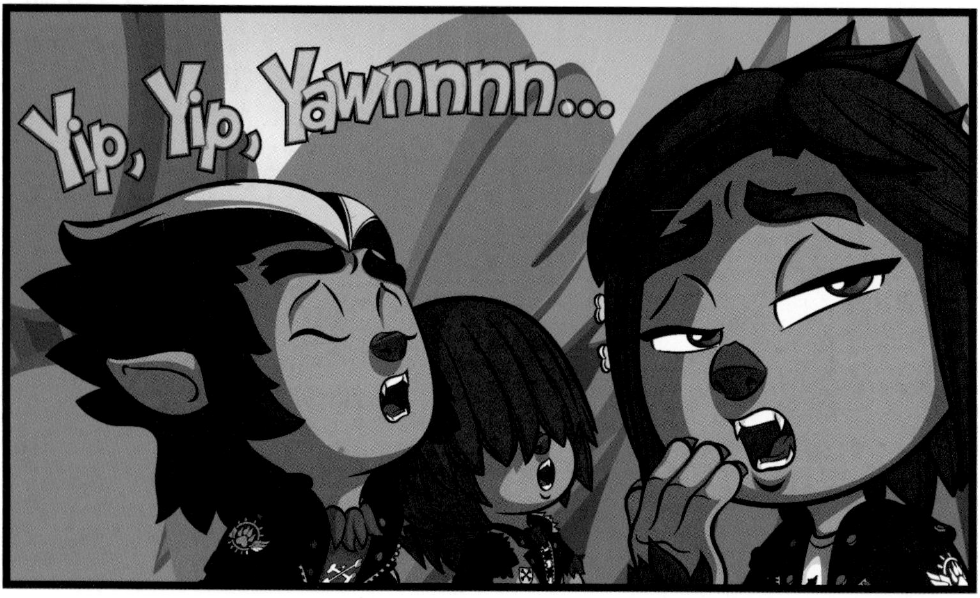
Yip, Yip, Yawnnnn...

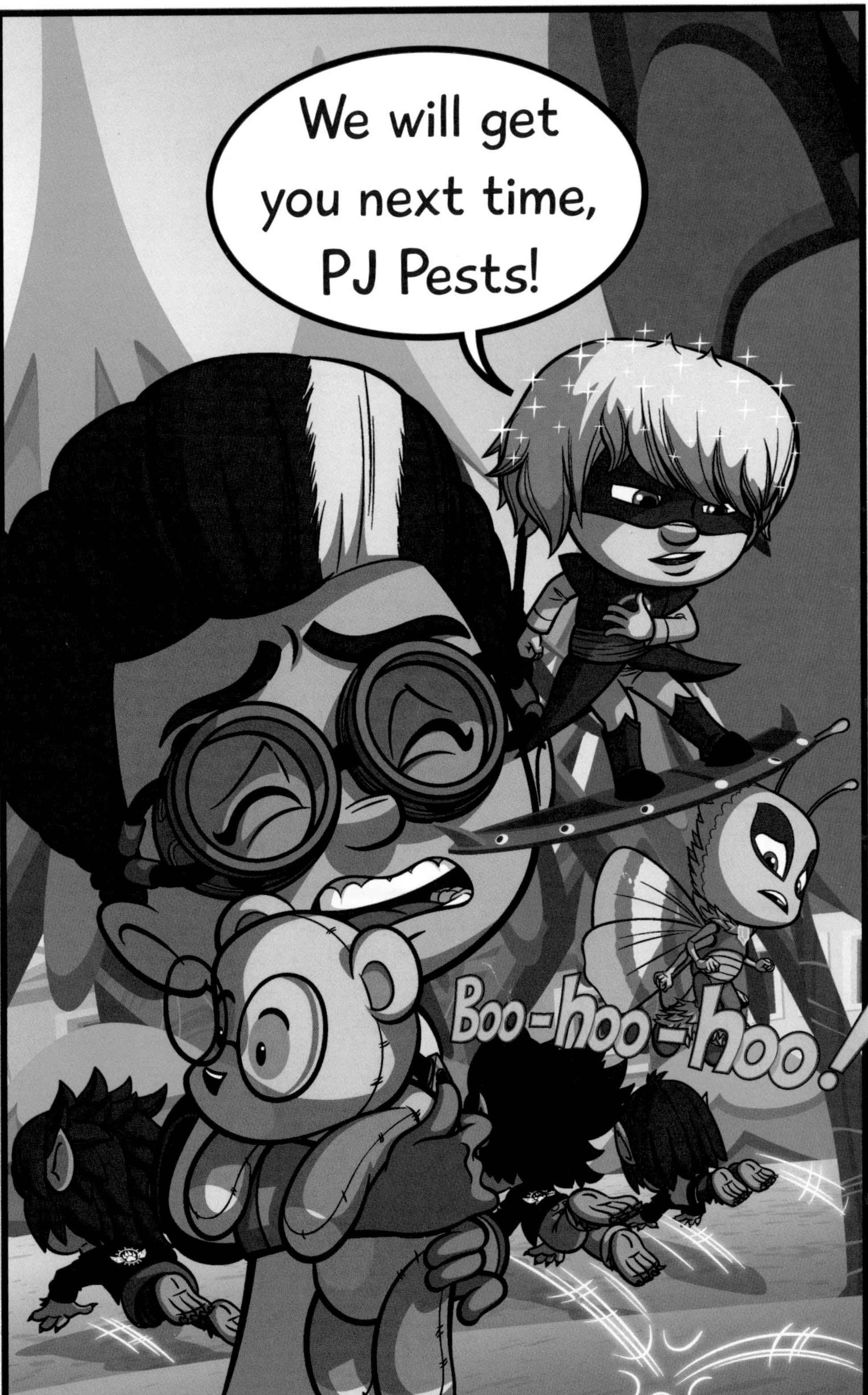
We will get you next time, PJ Pests!
Boo-hoo-hoo!

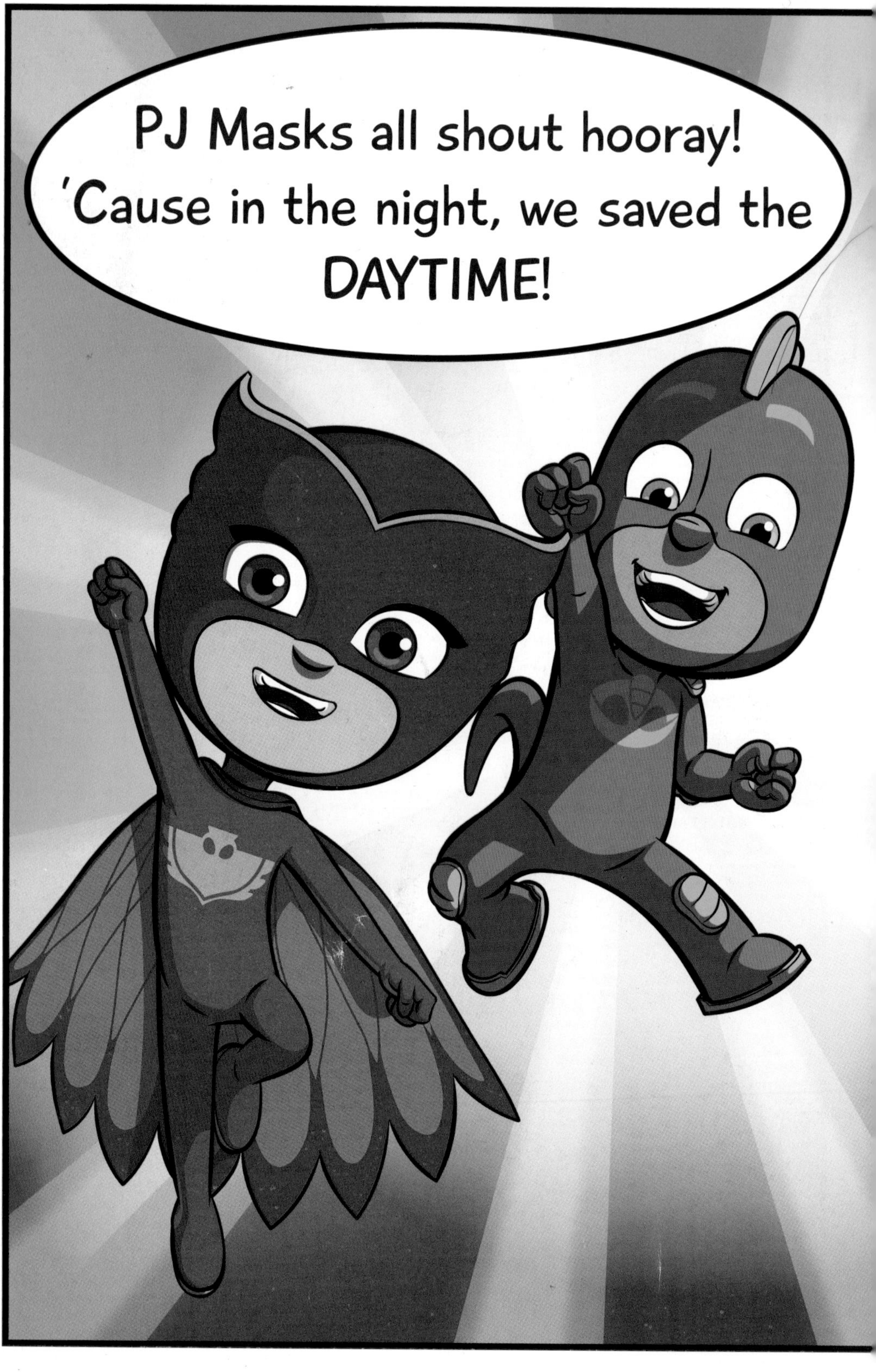
PJ Masks all shout hooray! 'Cause in the night, we saved the DAYTIME!

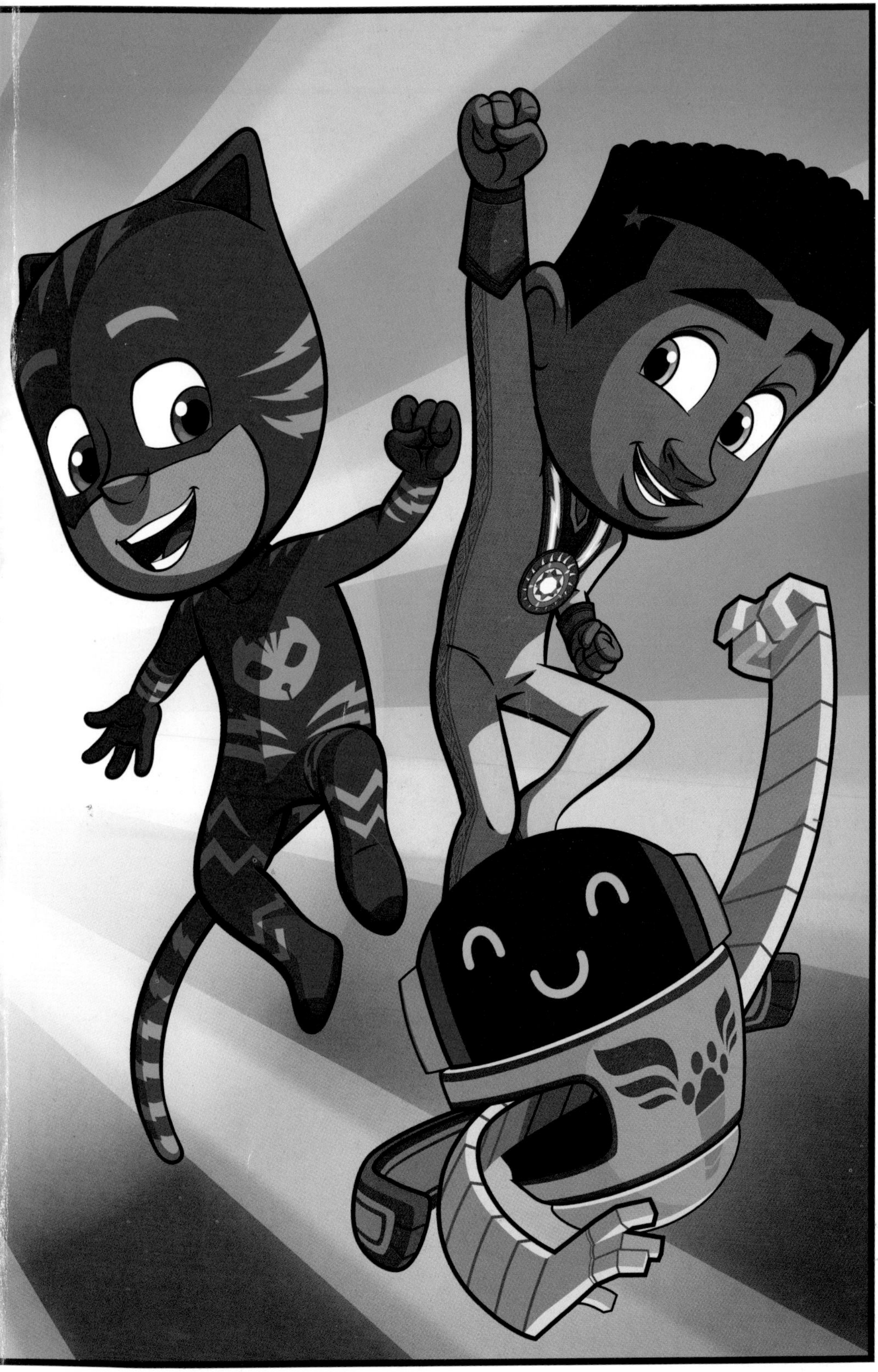

The next day at school...

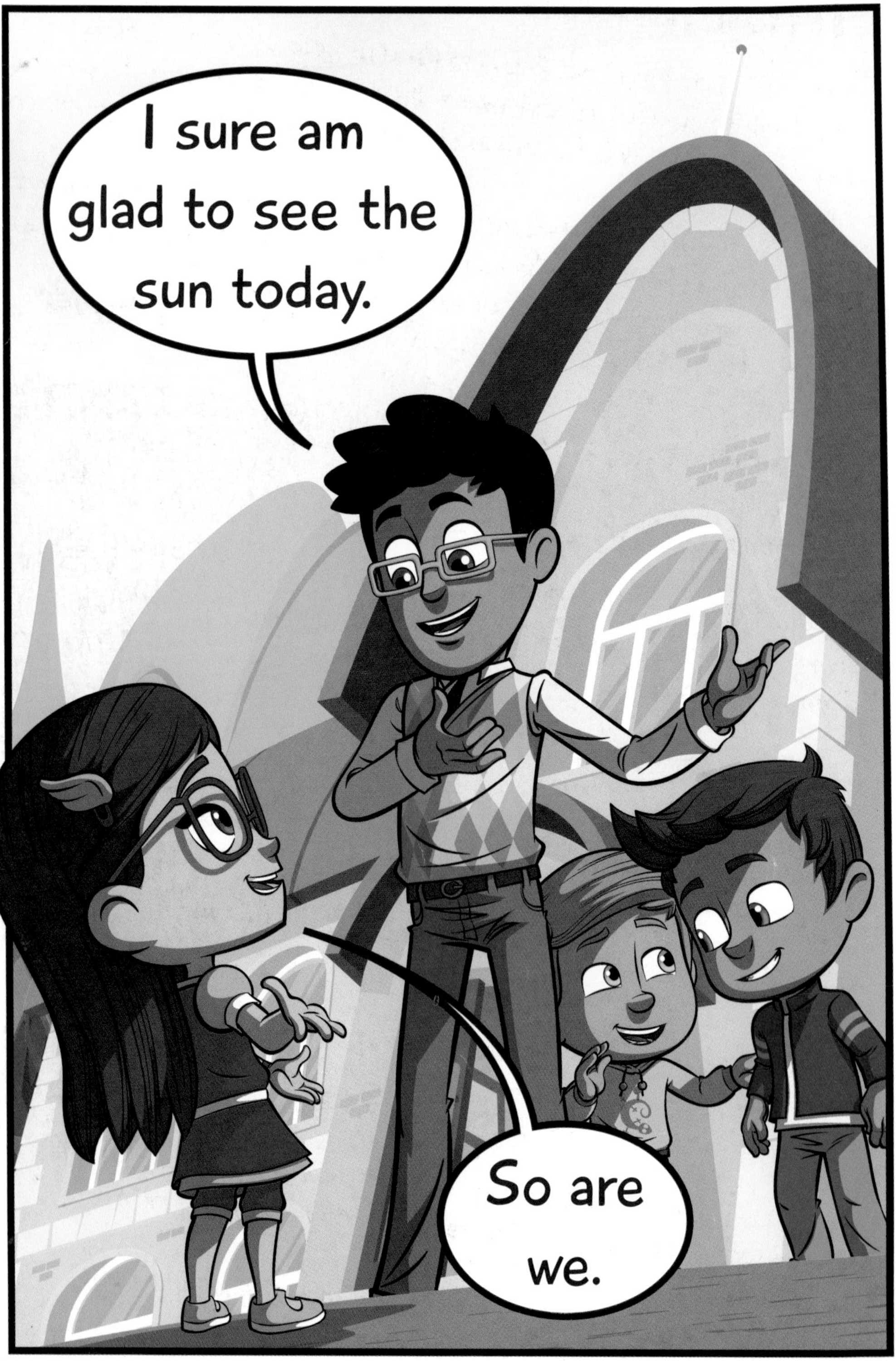
I sure am glad to see the sun today.
So are we.